No Charge
for Looking

No Charge for Looking

ESTHER COHEN

SCHOCKEN BOOKS • NEW YORK

First published by Schocken Books 1984
10 9 8 7 6 5 4 3 2   85 86 87
Copyright © 1984 by Esther Cohen
All rights reserved

Library of Congress Cataloging in Publication Data
Cohen, Esther.
  No charge for looking.
  I. Title.
PS3553.04196N6   1984   813'.54   84-1435

Designed by Cynthia Basil
Manufactured in the United States of America
ISBN 0-8052-3919-7

FOR P.O.

No Charge for Looking

One

Agram is the first sight in Nazareth. "No charge for looking," he bellows in front of the bus stop, repeating the sentence for each passerby. Both men and women stop for him. For the women, he follows his beseeching with "You are beautiful."

In June, Melanie Markowitz got off the bus. It was already too hot for her to descend with any grace, so she just got off, dropping her suitcase by her side and shaking her skirt free from the back of her legs. "No charge for looking," shouted a man in her direction. She looked up and saw him sitting on a small straw stool right in front of a kiosk of wood souvenirs.

Agram sells camels in olive wood, some with three humps just for luck, flamingos whose knees bend at perfect right angles, rosaries and Stars of David heaped together in a pile. His legs are a wide V, far apart and giving a hint of the breadth of his stance. He's big, with a more defined body than head. He has red hair and fading blue eyes, and even something like freckles: soft brown spots that fall over his face with an appealing randomness. He calls himself the Irish Palestinian, though he knows perfectly well there have been very few Irishmen there. His eyes are bulbous, visible even from a distance, with one wandering every so often to the right.

Melanie walked toward him, ready to sit down again. The ride from Tel Aviv was unsettling. She had shared her seat with a woman and her chicken. The woman seemed oblivious to the chicken, but

Melanie was not, holding onto her suitcase in mild fear that the chicken could somehow fly into her guidebooks and eat them.

"Take a load from your feet," said Agram to Melanie. He pulled out another straw stool from behind. She collapsed onto it, wilted by the journey. "I stayed over in Tel Aviv last night so I wouldn't be tired today," she began. "But I guess I still have jet lag. I feel very hot."

"If you didn't feel hot, you'd be dead," said Agram. "What will you have to drink?"

"Oh, no, thank you."

"Boy!" said Agram to no one in particular. A young boy appeared, balancing a yellow brass tray with what appeared to be the scale of justice resting in its center. "An orange and a tea." The boy held the tray on a line that was parallel to his head, in the middle of the air. "So," said Agram. "You are beautiful." This time he more clearly aimed his words at her.

"Thank you," said Melanie, who wasn't beautiful at all but had her moments. She was short and not yet wide, but her body's tendency to spread had already begun. Dark skirts de-emphasized this, and turtlenecks whenever possible. Today though she had chosen a Guatemalan blouse, not wanting to seem all that American. She wished there were a way to walk through the airport gates and instantly belong. That was one of the appeals Israel held for her. So many foreigners.

"You have beautiful eyes," said Agram, as if carrying on a conversation. He did not look at her directly, but seemed to be glancing over her shoulder in the general direction of the bus. Melanie sat with her back to the bus, so she couldn't tell what the subject of his interest really was. She was pleased to hear his compliment, though mildly suspicious. It was the kind of compli-she wanted to believe. Her eyes were her best feature, hazel and slanted up as if hers had been an interesting parentage. It hadn't, in fact: on both sides her family was Polish. "Are you French?" asked Agram.

"No," she said, pleased. "I was born in central New Jersey."

4

"New Jersey," said Agram. "I have a good friend there, a teacher of small children. Maybe you know her. Her name is Eileen."

"New Jersey is a big place," said Melanie. "I've been living in New York City for four years now. We're probably not acquainted."

"I have a letter from her," said Agram. He reached under his stool and drew out a cigar box closed with rubber bands. He opened it and revealed a pile of letters, neatly stacked, which he thumbed through, showing her postmarks from all over the world. He pulled out an envelope and handed her a sheet of stationery with *Eileen* emblazoned across the top in lilac. "Thank you thank you thank you," Eileen had written, "I've counted the thank-yous," said Agram. "More than one hundred. A very nice girl. Nice people in New Jersey."

"Some are nice and some aren't," said Melanie. "She sounds like a person who knows how to say thank you."

"They all do," said Agram, pulling out another letter. "This one is from Frankfurt in Germany," he said, handing it over. "A doctor. I told her I have problems to sleep, and she gave me some pills. Wonderful girl," he said.

Melanie glanced over the pages. The handwriting looked pinched. The sentences seemed to be written with the help of a ruler. One caught her eye: "I remember the way you caressed my vertebrae."

"She sounds intelligent," said Melanie.

"Do you speak in French?" said Agram. "I want you to see the beautiful letter from France. And look at the stamp. Everything over there is beautiful. Monique is a real girl," he said. The stamp showed a sketch of a woman with an especially pronounced nose. Melanie pulled out the letter, another testimony to undying love. *"Vous êtes mon Romeo,"* it read. Monique described lovemaking, but Melanie's French was from high school. "I asked them all to shave for me," said Agram to explain. "Clean is God. It's an expression I learned from an American. Wonderful girls, all of them." He put them back into the box neatly, securing them first with rubber bands. "These are hair souvenirs," said Agram. "I save everything."

Melanie was interested, almost against her better judgment. She didn't know any more than what the letter-writers had said: still, Agram seemed like a desirable man. It wasn't his looks, though he wasn't unattractive. Maybe it was the way he seemed impervious to the heat, a small yet important miracle. He sat, dry and untouchable, in the middle of Nazareth haze, facing the passersby with the stance of someone kingly. He wore a white shirt, loose and open, unbuttoned halfway down his chest. The shirt somehow heightened the sense of his size. The sleeves, cut off right above his elbows, seemed to emphasize the girth of his upper arms: they had the shape of a weight lifter's. Muscles protruded from the loose cotton, and yet his arms below the elbow were surprising: thin, hairless, fragile. His hands shifted back, though, resuming the largeness of his torso. They were baseball-glove hands: full, brown, lined. The tea, served in a juice-sized glass, looked small when he held it.

"Drink, drink," said Agram. "Don't you like your orange?"

"It's a little warm," answered Melanie. "Is there ice?"

"Do you think this is New Jersey?" he replied. "You're in Nazareth now. Why are you here?"

"I'm on assignment for a newspaper."

"The *New York Times*? They have been here many times."

"A much smaller paper called *American Journal.*"

He seemed to lose interest. "What do you do for a living?"

"I'm a journalist," said Melanie. "A writer. That's the reason I work for the *Journal.*"

"A writer," said Agram. "Will you write a book about me?"

She laughed. "What would you like me to say?"

"Say the truth," said Agram. "That's all I want. Just say who I am."

A woman turned a corner toward them, tall and full. She wore a sari and had four red dots across the center of her forehead. She was dark without being swarthy: creamy beige. Her hair was as black as an Indian's, and she wore it parted in the middle, pulled tight off her face, then woven into a long thick braid. The braid may have been fake, though it didn't look it at first. A navy blue line rimmed her eyes, and she'd painted a black beauty mark in the shape of a diamond right below her left cheek. "*Salaam aleykum* and welcome," she said to Melanie. "Are you from the States? I'm Cleo Joan Ginzburg," she said. "If you're wondering about these dots, I've been married four times. In India, the women wear dots instead of rings. I do both. Before I'm through, I'll probably look like a leopard. The last one almost finished me, though he was the one that died. I loved him. Don't get me wrong. For a hunchback he was a remarkable lover. But he had his bad side. What a temper! Sometimes he'd wake up in the middle of the night and just start shouting about the deplorable height of his pillow. It was always too high or too low to please him. At night he complained constantly, about the wrinkles on his sheets, or the unsatisfactory nature of his dreams."

"Why did you marry him?" Melanie asked.

"He was rich and persistent," she said. "And he had a chocolate factory. I've always been partial to a good candy bar. I loved him, but that came later. He could make me laugh if his mood was good, and as a lover he was one of the best."

"Not *the* best," said Agram. "He wasn't the best man you had." He looked worried.

"Just good," answered Cleo. "That's something, isn't it?"

"There are no men in America," Agram replied with assurance. "If you want a man, you have to come to Nazareth."

"We have men in America. I married four, and they were all from two states, Rhode Island and Connecticut. There are forty-eight states I have never even tried."

"The chocolate man was born in Argentina," said Agram, puzzled.

"But I met him in Rhode Island. I don't want to count Argentina. I've never been there. If you'd come to Rhode Island to visit, I could have met you there too."

"Why would I go there?" he said. "And besides, they don't know what a real man is over there."

"What is a real man? How is he different from the fakes?" Melanie asked.

"Slowly, slowly," said Agram. "We will help you to know."

"I'm from Providence," said Cleo. "I had a coffeehouse. The International Center for Coffee and Tea. Years before the House of

7

Pancakes. It was hard work, but it's how I met two of my husbands. They were customers.''

"Do you have any children?''

"Of course,'' answered Cleo. "Four. Four is my lucky number. There are three fours in my telephone number.''

"Where are they?''

"Aaron's in Wyoming making crepes at a ski lodge. He's a skier. He takes after his father. Joe was a tightrope walker, and Aaron is just as coordinated. Naomi is a junior in college. She's a psychology major. Her father is a Baptist minister, but he thinks of himself as a counselor. Che is in Mexico with Jorge. I loved Jorge too, but it didn't work. We got along best at work. He helped me serve. Lydia lives with her boyfriend in Vermont. They're in the carrot cake business. She is the daughter of the Argentinian, but you wouldn't know it. She'll only eat carob.''

"I didn't know you had children,'' Agram said, surprised.

"You never asked.''

"Do you have children?'' Agram asked Melanie.

"No, though I had a husband once. We've been divorced for two years now.''

"He made a living?'' Agram wanted to know.

"He was a linguist.''

"I can speak seven,'' he said. "Arabic, Hebrew, English, French and German. And Spanish and Italian.'' He looked pleased.

"A linguist does something else.''

"How many languages can he speak?''

"Two.''

"Aha,'' said Agram, victorious. "American men. Nothing. He can't make you happy. You don't love him.''

"I did,'' said Melanie. "When we got married I loved him very much.''

"So what did he do wrong?''

"She just didn't love him after a while,'' said Cleo.

"It wasn't that,'' answered Melanie.

"You people are hard to understand,'' said Agram. "That's what I liked about Eileen. She was easy.''

8

"We had different life-styles," said Melanie.

"What is life-style?" asked Agram.

Soundless, the same boy brought another tray of drinks, two oranges this time and a tea. He cleared what was there with a sweep of his hand. Agram ignored him. "Thank you, son," said Cleo.

"What are you doing here anyway?" asked Cleo.

"She's writing a book about me," answered Agram. "A big book. Don't worry. Your name is in it."

"What is the book's subject?"

"I'm not writing a book," answered Melanie. "It's just an article about Arabs. I work for a small American newspaper called the *Journal*, in New York. Someone left the paper a bequest to send a writer to Israel for three months to uncover what Palestinians are like. I'm here doing research."

"How will you go about it?"

"I arrived only yesterday," said Melanie. "I still have jet lag."

"She got off the bus at one P.M.," said Agram.

"It's already late," said Melanie, looking at her watch. It was 4:30 and the heat hadn't gotten any better. Her blouse, though loose, still seemed to stick to her like a wet handkerchief on a mirror. "I'm staying in town," she said. "With a woman I met once, when we were both children. Her mother and mine are friends from college. She's married to a man named Fuad Hassan."

"He went to college in America," said Agram. "In Michigan." He pronounced it like *Mitch*, slurring the end of the word so that for a minute Michigan sounded as if it were an Arab place.

"I am Jewish. Is she?" said Cleo. "Are you?"

"Yes," said Melanie.

"We are all brothers," added Agram. "Christian, Moslem, Jew, it's the same."

"Where do they live?" asked Cleo.

"On Frank Sinatra Street."

"Frank Sinatra was here to visit," said Agram. "He gave the Christians a center for boys."

"Can anyone go there?"

"To the gift shop," said Agram, "with souvenirs of Frank

9

Sinatra. They even have a dish with his picture. I bought one for the German doctor. She liked him. She has many of his records.''

"How did Frank Sinatra happen to come to Nazareth?"

"Sooner or later they all do," said Agram. "Sammy Davis, Jr. was here. Before he was Jewish. And Elizabeth Taylor and Hubert Humphrey. They've all been here. You're not the first one.

"We know about strangers," Agram continued. "Tomorrow we will take you. Maybe to the gift shop, maybe somewhere else. In the morning.''

"What if she has other plans?" asked Cleo.

"She wants us to take her.''

"Would you like to meet us tomorrow?"

"What do you ask?" said Agram. "Can't you see? I thought you were an intelligent woman. You had a business.''

"It's more polite," said Cleo.

"Why is polite better?" asked Agram.

"I would like to meet you both tomorrow," said Melanie.

"You see?" Agram looked at Cleo. "I know what I'm talking. Come to the Abu Nasser Cafe tomorrow," he said. "We will wait there for you. Don't worry, you will find it. Everything is very close.''

Two

It was a hot walk to Shari and Fuad's. Large-eyed children ran around her in circles. "You America?" they shouted, without waiting for her answer. She wondered why it was so obvious, even to them. "Hello," she'd say. "What's your name?" They would not answer.

The suitcases were too heavy. She shouldn't have taken all those books. "Can I help you, miss?" asked someone who looked very young. "Can I carry your luggage? Where is your final destination?"

"Fuad Hassan's."

"The Hassan family," said the young boy. "He studied in college in America. Are you from Michigan?" He said it in the same way as Agram, but it sounded better the second time. She handed over the luggage gratefully. "Where did you learn such good English?" she asked him.

"My teacher is from England. He is here," he said. "I have studied English for six years now. I want to go to college in America. Have you been to college?"

"Yes," said Melanie. "How old are you?"

"Seventeen," the boy said, then looked directly into the center of her face. "Almost," he amended. "My birthday is in several weeks. On the ninth of July I will be seventeen. But I consider myself as if already there. When did you arrive to our country?"

11

"Yesterday at noon," said Melanie. "I stayed overnight in Tel Aviv."

"How did you find it?"

"I took a taxi from the airport," answered Melanie.

"The city," asked the boy, "was it to your liking?"

"I walked around briefly," said Melanie. "I'm afraid I'm not a very good traveler."

"Neither am I," he responded. "I get tired even by a short voyage to Haifa. We have relatives there. My name is Fuad."

"Just like Fuad Hassan," said Melanie.

"It is a favorite name of our city," replied Fuad. "There are many of us in Nazareth. Fuad and Jesus are the two most popular. My family is Moslem, so Jesus was not possible. Jesus is Issa in Arabic."

"I see," said Melanie.

"Are there many of your name in your place of birth?"

"It is fairly common but not as common as others, like Susan, for instance."

"Do you know someone named Susan from California? She lives near the water."

"No," said Melanie. "California is one of the largest states in America."

"I see," said Fuad. "We all know our neighbors here." They walked down one dusty street after another. Women silently peered at them from doorways. The houses were hidden behind soft stone walls that seemed about to crumble.

"We are approaching the home of Fuad and Shari Hassan. And Mrs. Hassan," said Fuad.

"Does Fuad have two wives?"

"Only a mother. She is Christian, but her husband was Moslem. She is the owner of the villa."

"Is it a very big house?"

"There are five rooms. It is big enough for you to visit," answered the boy. "Don't worry. There is always room in Nazareth.

"What is your name?" he asked her. She told him, and he extended his hand with formality. "Very pleased to make your

12

acquaintance," he said. "If I can be of service during your stay here, do not hesitate to call upon me. Besides, it would be good practice for my English."

"I appreciate the kindness of your offer," said Melanie.

"Please take advantage of this opportunity," said Fuad. "I will introduce you to the Hassans, as an example of how I can be of help." He knocked on their door and said to the dark stranger who opened, "Allow me to present Miss Melanie Markowitz."

"Welcome," said Fuad. "We are expecting you."

"Good-bye," said Fuad. "Until we meet again."

"Melanie," squealed Shari. "You've finally arrived. We thought from your letter that you would be here yesterday. We waited up last night, then decided that the plane was delayed or that you'd postponed your leaving."

"Jet lag," said Melanie. "I am sorry I didn't call you from Tel Aviv, but I assumed you'd know that I would be here sooner or later."

"So you are," said Fuad. "So you are."

From a room on the side, a silent-looking, small, overweight woman appeared. She was all in black, a large cross swinging from her neck. "My mother is Catholic," said Fuad. "No English," said his mother softly. She looked down at the floor, but then moved her glance quickly to Melanie's shoes. They were canvas, shoe-polish white. They seemed to baffle Fuad's mother, whose expression changed from unhappiness to confusion.

"Come in," said Shari. "Would you like some tea or coffee? How about a cold drink? They drink tea when the weather's this hot, and it works. Would you like to try it?"

"I'll try anything," said Melanie. "I'm really hot."

Fuad's mother disappeared. Then the three of them sat in the cool sitting room. Furniture hugged the walls, which were cavelike but cheerful. A row of straight-backed light green chairs were lined up against one wall, as if in a waiting room. Opposite the chairs was a bed with pillows neatly arranged in a semicircle. "Sit on the couch," said Fuad pointing to the bed. He moved two chairs from the wall to the front of the bed, and opened a black TV tray. The TV tray had been painted by numbers. The painter had followed instructions carefully, leaving circles around the numbers themselves so the tree, a perfect green, had a circle with an 8 in its center. "Who painted this?" asked Melanie. "My mother," said Fuad. "She never stops working."

"We brought it to her from America," said Shari apologetically. "We couldn't explain about the numbers."

"She understood," said Fuad. "It's just that she likes it better like this. You've never believed that."

"How can she possibly like it better?" asked Shari. "It doesn't make any sense."

"She thinks it's more logical," said Fuad. "That way, people can see how she did it."

"Why would they want to?"

"Some people are curious," said Fuad. "Not everybody has answers to things."

"It's nice," said Melanie. "She did a neat job, if that was her intention."

"My mother is very neat," said Fuad.

"What is neatness if not mindless adherence to rules?" Shari asked.

"Order," said Fuad. "It's about order, and logic. Two things you are not capable of understanding."

"You'd like to believe that," said Shari. "Now, tell us why you came. Your letter was kind of vague."

"I'm working on a story," said Melanie. "I am a writer for a small newspaper in New York that randomly covers the world. Some years it's Latin America, others it's Southeast Asia. Now it's the Middle East. We got a small grant to write an article on Arabs in Israel, so the paper decided that I'd be the one to come. It's a collective," she explained. "They voted on me."

"Weren't you here before?" asked Shari.

"Yes," answered Melanie. "I came to Israel ten years ago for the summer, on a tour. We spent two weeks everywhere, but the country passed by me in a blur. All I remember about it is that I fell in love with someone in my group named Marvin Schline. He wore a hat all summer to protect himself from sunstroke."

14

"Have you been following the events of the country?"

"Yes and no," said Melanie. "I know several Israelis. I have a relative in Tel Aviv, a cousin of my father's. My family gets a New Year's card from him every year."

"And you have no real connection to the place?" asked Fuad. "Do you feel as though you can look at Nazareth with unbiased eyes, or do you have a preconceived point of view?"

"Give her a chance," said Shari. "She's a guest."

"I just want to see what she thinks."

"If she were smart, she wouldn't tell you."

"What's wrong with telling me? Maybe I could help her."

"Well, you're not going to help her if you make it seem as though you are adversaries. That isn't the way to establish a friendship."

"I haven't decided whether friendship is my goal."

"I'm only here to write a story," Melanie said, "not stop or start a war. Is the story so important?"

"Yes," said Fuad. "More than you know."

"Then maybe you could explain why, and I'll have a better understanding of your anxiety."

"Nothing is simple here," said Shari. "You just have to watch and see. Time moves slowly in Nazareth. Life takes longer than other places to understand."

"Do you like it here?"

"I have mixed feelings about our way of life," said Shari. "It isn't a good country for women, or Arabs."

"You're only one of those," said Fuad.

"Do you consider yourself both?" asked Shari.

"Why is it more difficult than anywhere else?" Melanie wanted to know.

"It has to do with the history of the peoples on the land, and the way that Israel affected its neighbors."

"It's who we are," said Fuad, "and what our choices are of becoming."

"Do you have any suggestions for how I can begin to find out about this life?"

"Keep your eyes open," said Fuad. "Just listen to everything around you. The more you hear, the better."

"Don't be easily influenced," said Shari. "Realize that in most places, there are two sides to every question. Here, there are at least three."

"Why three?"

"The Israelis, the Arabs, and the outsiders are part of every decision," said Shari.

"Do you consider yourself on a side?" asked Melanie.

"I'm an outsider who married into a side," said Shari.

"And is it a side you feel comfortable with?"

"Don't ask so much," said Fuad. "Watch. Sooner or later, you'll find out everything. And if you don't find it out, then maybe it isn't something you should know."

"Since when did you take such a spiritual approach to politics?"

Fuad's mother reappeared again, as soundlessly as she'd left. Her voice was a whisper in Fuad's direction. It seemed to be about urgent matters. She bent over as she spoke to him, leaning with the top of her body like a sailor on a moving boat. Fuad seemed attentive to her, and concerned.

"I never have any idea what they're discussing," said Shari. "I've been studying Arabic for years now, but Fuad's mother speaks so quietly that I can't even hear her."

"Do you know what the subject of their conversation is?"

"It's always food," said Shari. "They talk about what to eat, and when. She consults him on all matters of cooking. And when she doesn't, he complains. He is her culinary secretary of state."

"Does Fuad cook?"

"He knows what it should taste like, more than how to make it. He can cook a few dishes. Fuad says everything I make tastes like hamburgers."

"Do you miss American food?"

"Once in a while. I have gotten very used to this life. Though I don't belong in Nazareth quite, living here has made me feel as though I don't belong anywhere else either."

"Do you go back to visit?"

"We write," said Shari. "Sooner or later we will take a trip. My father refuses to acknowledge Fuad. He writes notes on the bottom of

16

my mother's letters, saying 'Hello to *you*.' He underlines the *you*, to make sure I know he isn't saying hello to anyone else. My mother sends me designer sheets, but she's never come to visit. She wants our beds to look like home. Every two years she sends different-colored towels. My father doesn't know she sends them. One thing I miss here is having women friends.''

''What are the women like?''

''Arab women tend to be subservient. If they're not, then they leave. The Israelis treat me as though I'm a white married to a black in Selma, Alabama. I went to a women's meeting in Haifa a few years ago. In the beginning of the session the leader went around the room and asked us all to give a quick sketch of our lives. 'What's it like being married to them?' she asked me. I felt as though I'd married an entire people.''

''What is it like?''

''I would have done anything at all to escape from the dullness of my surroundings growing up. The whole world seemed made out of Styrofoam cups. And Fuad was a revolutionary.''

''What does he do now?''

''He's still a revolutionary, but he's working in his uncle's bridal store. He thinks weddings are only mildly reactionary. And he's writing an epic novel he hopes to sell to Hollywood.''

''What do you do here?''

''I work in an experimental Arab-Jewish nursery school. So far, only Arab children come, but every year we hope that the situation will change.''

''Do you think it will?''

''One thing about life in Nazareth, you never can tell what will happen. In some ways, I got what I wanted. It's constantly changing in ways I can't fathom. Day to day, the possibilities vary. I find that exciting.''

''So do I,'' said Melanie. She felt a little overwhelmed.

Three

Agram and Cleo were waiting for Melanie when she got to their cafe, the Abu Nassar, early the next morning. They looked as though they'd been sitting for hours, though it was still early when she arrived. The Formica tables, newly washed, were already approaching dusty, and the day was unbearable from the start. The tables were close together, like tables and chairs for children in an old-fashioned ice-cream parlor. It was almost as though overhearing were an acknowledged intention of their placement. The customers seemed to be listening and talking at once. They spoke, conscious of audiences that weren't necessarily restricted to those they could see. Agram addressed the other patrons as he spoke to the women. "Today you will see everything," he seemed to say to the morning coffee drinkers, all men. Cleo and Melanie smiled at him, almost at once. "We will begin with a special surprise. I will take you to my factory."

"I didn't know you had one," said Melanie.

"You see," answered Agram, pleased, "I told you it was going to be a surprise."

"What do you make in your factory?"

"You say it, we sell it," said Agram. "An American with a lot of money told me that."

"Olive wood," said Cleo. "It's a specialty of the area. They make olive-wood souvenirs."

"A zoo we have there," said Agram. "Camels, dogs, cats, even a lion. Imagine a lion made out of olives."

19

"He isn't made out of olives," said Cleo.

"Have you seen the lion?"

"No," said Cleo. "But I know he isn't made out of olives."

"Wait, wait," said Agram. He raised his hand with the same sense of commanding purposefulness as the day before, only this time he snapped his fingers. The sound was soft rather than crackling, as if sliding his thumb across his middle finger was all that was needed. A big old black car with a broken side door and a mermaid hood ornament pulled up to the cafe. Tassled curtains were drawn across the side and back windows, and a china cat with a moving head peered out from the back window ledge. The driver looked as dusty as the car, but he was smiling. He was dressed like Agram, in a very loose shirt in a color that was almost white but not exactly, and black pants tipped with pointed shoes. "How ya doin'?" he said to all three. His pronunciation was nearly American. "I been following football in your country." He smiled at Melanie as though this would please her. *Football* sounded like *food ball* when he said it.

Agram introduced him as Bobby. "His given name is Jesus, but he liked John F. Kennedy," Agram explained. Bobby held the back door open for the women and stood at attention as Agram climbed in front. Then they slapped each other's hands and winked.

"Where shall we take these American chickens?" asked Bobby knowingly.

"You know where," answered Agram. He laughed. Cleo was smiling.

"Aren't we going to the factory?" asked Melanie.

"Don't worry your small head," answered Bobby. "Leave it to the men in the car."

They drove through downtown Nazareth. Suddenly, Bobby put on the brakes. The car stopped by bouncing up in the air. "Upsy daisy," said Bobby.

"He was married to an American," said Agram. "They lived in Haifa."

Bobby jumped out of the car. He ran to the back door and let Cleo out first. Then Melanie: with a broad gesture downward, he bent forward, swept his arm out as though he were the chauffeur. They walked into a musty cave where men sat at long stone tables. It

20

looked like a mead hall at first. There was very little light, an intense smell of wood. Too much noise filled the big room, a buzzing and shouting, with the general feeling that something more was happening than met the eye.

Agram walked from man to man, patting each on the back heartily, knocking the wind right out of some. They all seemed smaller than he was. He winked to them, one by one, acting brotherly. The women stood against the wall. Cleo waved hello to the men, with a very tentative gesture. She raised her right hand, but only as high as her shoulder. She seemed to be surveying the contenders for possible husband number five. One of the tables of workers was turning out olive-wood TV sets, to be used as salt and pepper shakers. They carved three different things on the TVs: Golda Meir. Billy Graham, and Kojak. The carver gave Melanie a pair of Goldas. "Thank you," she said shyly.

"My Misses America," Agram said to both the women, "anything here is yours." He pointed in the direction of an elaborate lamp, olive wood carved like a big deer with antlers. Instead of resting on top of the deer, the light bulb came from its mouth. "Forty-five dollars U.S.," said Agram, pointing to the deer. "It's yours if you say so."

"Just give him the word," said Bobby.

"The car is ready, Agram," said Bobby. He hadn't left the cave, yet somehow he knew.

"She's seen enough for today, dear," said Cleo sweetly. "You don't want her to have more than she can digest."

"Lunch," said Agram. "That reminds me of lunch."

"That's right," said Bobby. "My stomach is making a noise for a sandwich."

Bobby's car moved along, back in the direction of the cafe.

At lunch, Agram asked Melanie questions, not about her but about Fuad and Shari. "So what is this man like?" he asked. "I know the answer, but I want to hear your good English."

"Why are you so interested in Fuad?" asked Cleo. "Don't you know him?"

"He is my brother."

"For a brother you don't seem to know each other too well," said Melanie.

"We are all brothers. Arabs, Israelis, Americans, Germans."

"What about the women?" asked Melanie.

"You don't understand," Agram sounded petulant. "I mean everybody. All are brothers. Even you."

Cleo and Melanie laughed. "He's using the term loosely," said Cleo.

"What's the matter?" asked Agram. "You are not my brother?"

"I am," said Melanie. "I am also your sister."

"Aha," said Agram. "I see. So tell me something from this Mr. Fuad and Shari, his American wife."

"What would you like to know?"

"He wants to know anything you can tell him," said Cleo. "His curiosity is insatiable."

"Maybe you should meet him," suggested Melanie. "I'd be happy to arrange it. That is, if you'd like to have a chance to form your own impressions of his character."

"Do you like him?" asked Agram. "Are you in love with him?"

"She hardly knows him," said Cleo. "What are you asking?"

"She knows," said Agram. "Well?" he turned to Melanie.

"I hardly know him," she said. "Besides, he's happily married."

"You are very young," said Agram.

"What do you mean by that?"

"I mean you can love him married."

"Why would I?"

"You mean you don't?"

"Agram, you are being ridiculous," said Cleo. "Of course she doesn't love him. And what difference does it make to you?" Cleo said this as if she knew very well what love was, from her current circumstance. She touched his arm.

"Chemicals," replied Agram. "There is always a chemical." He stared at Cleo briefly, then smiled at Melanie. Melanie could see very clearly that Cleo and Agram, for instance, were in love. At least, Cleo seemed in love with Agram, and Agram, in his way, seemed in love with Cleo too. This made sense, but it also made

22

Melanie mildly jealous. She wondered how it would feel to be loved by a man like Agram, and how it would feel to love him.

"Tell us about Shari," said Cleo. "Do you know her well?"

"I met her once when we were children," Melanie replied. "She is a feminist. That's all my mother told me before I came here. And she seems to have had a difficult life."

"What is feminist?" asked Agram.

"A woman who believes that her sex is a political issue." Melanie wasn't sure exactly how to answer him.

"What kind of issue?"

"She feels that she's been oppressed because she's a woman," explained Melanie. "Her life has been profoundly affected by her sex."

"And men," asked Agram. "Our life is not?"

"Yes, but men are in the position of control. Feminists want to share the control," said Melanie.

"It's not an easy idea for a Middle Eastern man," claimed Cleo. "You are used to thinking of yourself as a king."

"All men do," said Melanie. "The difference is that in some parts of the world that idea is evolving."

"There are places where women are kings?" asked Agram.

"No," said Melanie. "There are places where men and women both recognize the difficulty that history's created. They are making a serious effort to change."

"What do you think of this, Cleo?" asked Agram.

"I think," said Cleo, "that control and power are difficult matters to dissect. But it's about time the situation changed."

"You had four husbands." Agram sounded angry. "Would you have had them if you weren't a woman?"

"I wouldn't have needed them," said Cleo.

"Shari seems both serious and lost. I suppose those are not opposite qualities at all."

They continued talking for some time, and when they parted Agram asked Melanie if she would arrange for a dinner with her friends. "I must meet them again," he said. "Even if I know them already."

Four

Shari was anxious to meet a woman from Providence, and Fuad was
curious about Agram. They only knew each other by reputation.
When Fuad went away to America, Agram was already married with
children. By the time he returned, their lives were not connected by
anything except the town, and though Fuad saw Agram occasionally
walking by his uncle's shop, they rarely spoke. Fuad felt Agram was
the kind of man who could help with a revolution.

The restaurant was one of those places that are only in the Middle
East, small and spare and timeless and almost holy. There were no
immediately visible colors in the room, no obvious furniture. Several
men were sitting together in a corner on stools. They seemed to be
mumbling. The feeling was an odd one, of both eternity and tran-
sience. John F. Kennedy, on a rug, ringed by dancing deer, smiled
out from the wall, a friend to Arabs. So did a bright blue Elvis
Presley, but the Kennedy rug was bigger. The only sign of active life
was music, constant and high, a shrill and familiar wail. More than
Chinese or Indian music, which sound similar to it at first, Arabic
music comes from somewhere deep in a soul that's suddenly emerg-
ing.

Shari and Fuad and Melanie arrived first. Fuad did the speaking.

"Fawzi, how are you?" he said to the owner.

"And you, Mr. Fuad. This must be your beautiful Jewish wife."

"I am only half Jewish," said Shari, irritated.

"Was it your mother?" asked Fawzi.

"Yes," answered Shari, "and she was the dominant one in our household."

"We are all brothers," responded Fawzi automatically.

"You all repeat that all the time," said Shari. "What about sisters?"

"I am tired of hearing that," said Fuad. "Why do you insist on meaningless changes of language?"

"Would you like to be one of the gals?" asked Shari. "Would you feel included if I repeated that we are all sisters day in and day out?"

"What difference does it make?" asked Fuad. "They are only words."

"We love women here," responded Fawzi. "All women. Danish, French, Jewish, American. Anything that moves on two feet."

"I have to go to the bathroom," said Shari, restraining herself for the sake of the evening.

"Are you pregnant?" asked Fawzi. "It's time."

"That's none of your business," answered Shari.

"American women are very strange," said Fuad, winking to Fawzi in an all-knowing way.

"I know, I know." Fawzi smiled. Then he raised his entire head to the ceiling, as if asking for comprehension from above. "The room is there, for ladies, girls, sisters, all of them."

Shari left, moving her hips in an exaggerated gesture, broadly sweeping left to right.

"Fawzi, I'd like to introduce our guest," said Fuad. "She's an American journalist here on assignment."

"For what paper do you work?"

"You've never heard of it."

"It's not in Los Angeles, by any chance? I have a cousin there."

"It's in New York."

"A very big city, that New York. Crime all over the place. When you walk down the streets, you are afraid."

"It's a place that's not without interest," said Fuad. "Unique in the world, like Nazareth."

"Yes," said Fawzi. "I know all about it. We have prepared a table especially for you," he said. "We want you to have a real

Arabic meal tonight. You've never had food like this before, and unless you come back, you'll never have it again.''

"I'm looking forward to eating."

"I have prepared some specialties, so you don't have to go through the trouble of ordering."

"Americans don't know about eating," said Fuad. "When I went to Michigan, my mother sent me food in the mail. They eat plastic. All they know how to make are the cakes. Sarah Lee. Do you eat them?" he asked Melanie.

"Yes," she answered. "Do you like the chocolate fudge?"

"Orange," he replied. "It is better. The oranges are real."

"It's a fast-food society," Melanie explained. "No one has the time to prepare."

"But what are you women doing all day?" asked Fawzi.

"Don't start," said Fuad.

"You know I love them all," said Fawzi. "My wife is in the kitchen. You will meet her."

Shari came back. "Can we sit down?" she asked.

"Of course, my Mrs. Hassan," he said.

"Kliger," said Shari. "I use my maiden name."

"Of course, Mrs. Kliger," he replied.

"Where is Agram?" asked Fuad.

"He shouldn't be late," Melanie told them. "He wears two watches at once, a Timex and a Rolex. He's an international Timex tester. Every two years, he gets one for free."

"Where did he get the Rolex?" asked Fuad.

"I don't know," said Melanie. "Maybe a wealthy admirer. He seems to have many women who write to him."

"Is he attractive?" asked Shari.

"I'm not sure," said Melanie. "Although he must be if so many women have succumbed."

"Maybe it's just a question of circumstance," said Fuad. He sounded jealous.

"Or charisma," said Shari. "He could have an appeal that transcends cultures."

"I met many women in Michigan," said Fuad.

27

"I know that," said Shari. "I was one of them."

"Do you think people pay less attention to time in the Middle East?" Melanie asked them. "Does being on time mean less here than in America?"

"We have more of it," answered Fuad. "We are a leisurely people. We have spent many years thinking. Like the Japanese, we know there is no need to rush."

"The Japanese are in a constant hurry," answered Shari. "Here you're used to sitting. Everyone sits. TV is a natural."

"You are wrong, dear Shari," said Fuad. "You misinterpret our patience for passivity. In fact, we are on the verge of a serious breakthrough."

"What sort?" Melanie asked. "What will happen after the breakthrough?"

"The action will take place in an interior fashion," said Fuad. "With serious exterior consequences. We are an ancient people, readying ourselves for eternity. Have you ever watched a ball of string unravel?"

"But there's nothing at the center."

"You'd be a very good journalist," said Fuad. "You see the point quickly."

"But how can a society develop toward nothing?"

"An Oriental mystery," said Fuad. "We all believe that in the East. It's an older world here. We understand what life is, because we can feel it."

"Can you see now how attractive I find the way here?" said Shari. "I fight against it, but in the end I give in."

Fawzi walked to the table very slowly. His feet seemed to move in spite of his sandals, slipping forward with a slow shuffling sound. The sandals looked held onto his arches by invisible strings. His pants were very loose. He looked smooth, unruffled, cool in the evening heat.

"I have a message for this table," he announced. "Agram has telephoned. He will be here momentarily. He is on his way. A very important business matter has detained him. I have known Agram since he was a boy."

"How old is he now?" Melanie asked.

"Impossible to say. He is ageless and timeless."

"How much younger is he than you?" Shari tried.

"If I knew that, I could answer your friend's question, my dear girl," said Fawzi. "Let's drink some arak together while we are waiting. It is a very special drink. Do you know it?" he asked Melanie.

"No," she answered. "But I am willing to try anything."

Flies entered and circled the ceiling in droves. They were more like minnows than flies in their numbers. Suddenly, the door opened and the night seemed to cool the hot room all at once. Everything became dark, then light, then dark again. Agram walked in, smiling, with Cleo. Bobby was close behind.

"You know, people thought the esteemed Christopher Columbus was crazy for thinking the world wasn't flat," said Fuad to Shari and Melanie. They looked at him questioningly. "It is hard to understand what you see there," he said.

Agram walked toward them slowly. The other two had shifted positions. Bobby was by his side, and Cleo followed. Agram smelled of allspice and lemons, and this preceded him by seconds. He was three-dimensional, a master of creating his own importance.

"I'm coming from a meeting, about what I can't tell you. Maybe another time," he said. He winked at Bobby. Cleo smiled. Everyone shook hands. The proprietor stepped forward. "I have made a very special meal," he announced for the second time.

"There is nothing like your cooking, George," said Agram, taking over.

Fawzi laughed. "He has always called me George. The cooking is my wife's."

"A beautiful girl," said Agram. "The cousin of Bobby's wife."

"This wife is beautiful," said Bobby. "But I was more crazy about the American. She had problems, that girl. This one doesn't have a care in the world. The American wanted to learn to fly airplanes."

"Why was that a problem?" asked Shari.

"Because there are no airplanes in Nazareth," said Bobby.

"So couldn't she go to Tel Aviv to learn?"

"Why do you always complicate things?" said Fuad. "Maybe he doesn't want to tell you what her problem was."

"I will tell you," said Bobby. "She wanted to fly."

"You Americans," said Agram. "Always causing problems. We have enough by ourselves."

"You mean you don't like us?" asked Melanie.

"Of course he likes us," answered Cleo. "If he didn't like us he wouldn't be here."

"I am glad to meet you," said Agram to Fuad and Shari. "Your guest is a very nice girl. So how do you like our country now, Miss America?"

"I find it mysterious," she answered. "It's hard for me to have much sense of what's going on here, though I've read a lot of the literature at home. And a few descriptive articles."

"Wait until I finish my novel," said Fuad. "It is a sweeping epic, explaining everything, Arabs, Jews, Christianity, Islam, and Mao."

"It's not in the books," said Agram. He smiled as if he knew more than anyone else ever could. Agram imparted a sense of wisdom that seemed available for a very high price. "Before too long," he said, "you may be able to know what's the story. Before too long you'll have the answers for your America." He smiled again, confident. When he smiled his face looked ageless, his hair seemed to grow more thick on the spot. His gestures were carefully noted by everyone watching him. He was not a handsome man, but he was compelling, desirable, larger than life. He had a secret, and it was his secret that made others want to know who he was. It was all a part of his physical presence, his sex, his strength, the shape of his hands.

Melanie appeared more and more drawn to him. He talked to her with an intensity that seemed to grow by the sentence, not in words, but in feelings.

"I don't read the newspapers," he said to her. "How can you write about anything in such short sentences, such few words? Israelis write about other Israelis. I don't even know if they like each other. For them, there are few good Arabs. We are always blowing up houses, buses, schools, and people, planting bombs in the paths

30

of schoolchildren or worse. Occasionally, one of us manages to win their national lottery. They write about us then. Then we are good citizens. We are contributing to their country. We are like wives, with no life of our own. Whatever we do is dependent on another person's idea for us. We can leave, but it would be leaving our homes. They are not real to us either. We see them, but they are in uniform, watching us as if any minute we will try to destroy them." His voice sounded as though he were about to explode. "Our feelings don't count for you," he said. "You don't know who we are, and you don't want to know. You feel that knowing us will somehow threaten your own self."

"That's not true," said Melanie. "I want to know."

"What about me?" said Cleo. "I know already. So does Shari."

"I am talking about Melanie," said Agram. "I'll bet you didn't see any Palestinians in your New York."

"That's unfair," said Cleo. "We all know people like ourselves."

"But you didn't," said Agram. "You married four different men."

"That was something else," said Cleo. "Circumstance. Where are your Israeli friends?"

"Some Arabs and Jews are friends, but this is different," he replied. "There's a war here."

"We are all victims of our class limitations," said Fuad. "An Israeli academic and a Palestinian academic have a good chance of meeting, particularly if they are both in the same field. There are many in Middle East politics, for instance."

"They will meet in New York," said Agram. "Or Paris, or Rome."

"Your wonderful dinner is ready at last. I bring you lamb," said Fawzi.

Everyone ate, hearing explosions in the distance like very loud fireworks, followed by a shattering sound. It was loud and close.

"That's nothing," said Agram. "Just noise of the Nazareth night. We're used to it. The noise is older than you are."

"Do you know who it is? Who is fighting? Israelis or Arabs?"

31

Melanie became afraid. "How can you tell?"

"I felt like you when I first heard explosions," said Shari. "Don't worry. If they're nearby, there's nothing you can do. If they are far away, they'll never reach us. No one wants to kill Americans anyway. We are only dangerous when we're dead."

"How will they know where we are?" asked Melanie.

The restaurant owner seemed engaged in elaborate ballet. He tiptoed back and forth bringing dishes, smallish plates with green and red and brown minced objects on all of them. It was hard to tell what they were.

"Eat," he said. "So how do you like my wife's cooking?" he asked a minute later.

"Your wife should have been mine," said Fuad.

"It's not too late. When Shari leaves, we will make a deal." The men laughed.

"Don't be so sure I'm leaving," said Shari.

"Why can't you learn to cook like an Arab?" asked Fuad. "Ask my mother."

"Your mother's English is minimal. She's a good cook, but she doesn't want to show me how."

"It's hardly minimal. And she reads 'Dear Abby' in Arabic translation."

"An odd choice."

"She wants to know what your people are thinking, in the same way you want to know her thoughts. Besides, Abby is a Christian," said Fuad.

"That's what you think," said Shari. "How did your mother come to that conclusion? I don't think your mother ever made a real effort to understand me."

"Shari, you are only interested in demeaning my mother," said Fuad. "You feel she's impinging on your territory. We are all impinged upon. It is an impossible part of this life."

"Untrue," claimed Shari. "Look at Agram. No one is impinging."

"Have I ever told you the joke about the Egyptian and the Syrian?" said Agram.

Five

Cleo and Melanie met alone one morning at the cafe. Agram was in Jerusalem on business. Cleo was always totally different: an Indian bride, an African tribeswoman, a Japanese geisha, an American stewardess. The day she told Melanie about Agram, she was a Thai dancer. She wore long golden brass covers over her forefingers, pointed and curling. Her dress was a red silk sarong, tightly wound around her body Dorothy Lamour style, and she had attached a large white flower to her hair. As usual, she looked as though she belonged somewhere else.

Melanie was already starting to look better herself. Her skin was less dry than when she'd first arrived, and the excitement of being in a foreign country added new sparkle to her eyes. She'd replaced the tiny gold balls in her ears with silver coins from Turkey that dangled from chains. She wore a wraparound denim skirt and a Yemenite blouse that an aunt had brought her from Israel years before. It was pretty, white with careful blue embroidery. They looked happy talking to each other.

"He doesn't like us to meet without him," said Cleo. "He's afraid we might assess the situation or compare notes. But he couldn't help going away today, and if he took us with him, we'd probably understand what he was doing there. He likes keeping his life shrouded in mystery. For Agram, mystery is more important than anything."

"What is the lure of mystery for him?"

"He uses it as technique," said Cleo. "Women love him for it. Men think he's more important than they are. It's so much easier to love what's unfamiliar. You have another chance in a place where you don't know the rules, or what will happen at the outset, so you suppose your fantasies will actually work. I felt that way with all of my husbands, and I feel it with Agram too. Though I can see him pretty clearly, still he comes from a world that's unknown to me. And because it's unknown, I find it easier to love."

"You don't mind that he's already married?"

"Yes, I mind," said Cleo. "I have always been the jealous type. But I also have Nathan."

"You have someone besides Agram?"

"Nathan is only a sexual partner," said Cleo. "It means nothing. Besides, he enjoys walking. I don't do any other exercise, like swimming or tennis. I like going for a walk every day. Here they are suspicious if you walk by yourself. Everyone assumes you're a prostitute. Men keep accosting you, and women give you dirty looks."

"Does Agram know?"

"Are you crazy?" said Cleo. "He would kill me. Agram doesn't like competition. We go walking in the Jewish part of Nazareth. Nathan's an Indian Jew. We both live there. Agram only knows what happens in his part of town. He's not allowed to sit and watch in the other section."

"What's Nathan like?"

"Let's go to see him. You should visit Upper Nazareth anyway. The chocolate factory is there, and the shopping mall. Nazareth is a divided city, and the two parts are totally different. It's like meeting two men named Asher. They don't necessarily have much in common, except for the oddity of their name."

They took a green bus up a winding hill that revealed one miraculous vista after another each time the driver turned a corner. He put on the gas as he turned, as if to accelerate the view. He smiled at Cleo through his mirror, and she smiled back. "I come up and down all day," she said. "So he knows me."

The other passengers, mostly women, gave Cleo and Melanie glances of mistrust. Although they, too, had boarded the bus in Arab Nazareth, they were suspicious of anyone else doing the same. There were two kinds of women riders: overweight peasants, grasping fishnet bags bulging with bread that looked like fattened French loaves, and city ladies from Europe. These had pocketbooks, neat and modern, stylish clothes that tightly hugged their bodies, beautiful hair and new shoes, high and open-toed. The few men were older, like wizened Greek fishermen, with gray wool cardigans under their suit jackets and navy blue caps pulled down tight on their brows. Cleo and Melanie were clearly outsiders. The ride took only a few minutes, but when they got off it was obvious they'd come to a very different place from where they'd been. It was modern suddenly, new and clean, with very wide streets like in Kansas City. The town was all on top of a hill, overlooking valleys and villages. The houses looked as though they'd been made from a Lego set. They nested on top of each other like an Escher painting, perfectly equidistant, giving the impression that their inhabitants were very neat, the sort of people who alphabetize their spices.

"It's beautiful here," said Melanie. "The whole town seems built into the rocks. It reminds me a little of Mykonos."

"All new," said Cleo. "There are parks everywhere. More than in Providence. And views. Everyone has a view of something."

"What a wonderful place to live."

"Under the right circumstances," said Cleo.

Nathan's apartment was half a block from the bus stop. As they approached, they heard a Jimi Hendrix song playing inside.

"I wonder where he got that album," said Melanie.

"Nathan is a man of surprising resources," said Cleo.

"Come in come in come," said Nathan in a voice that sounded singsong British. He looked like an Indian Efrem Zimbalist, Jr. His hair was long and wet, slicked back and wavy. He was the type of man whose comb is never far from his hand.

"This is a friend from America," Cleo told him.

"Another American. There are a great many of you here," he

said. "You are most welcome indeed. We need you Americans for your technical know-how. You are also famous for your jazz. Are you a musical individual?"

"No," said Melanie. "But I do like music. How did you first hear about Jimi Hendrix?"

"I saw him in London," said Nathan. "My brother has a Cash and Curry restaurant there. His name is Mr. Shreedar Burda."

"Are there many Jews in India?"

"We all know each other," said Nathan, in an up-and-down voice. "We live in the south. Many are here now. We came to Israel in the late fifties. My family arrived together, but some have gone. One is even in your country in dry goods. Indians are like Jews. They are all over. Indian Jews are twice as prone to wander."

"How old are you?" Melanie asked him.

"Thirty-seven, but I look twenty-five," he said.

"Nathan, will you walk us through the town?" asked Cleo. "Melanie has never been here before."

"Why, of course," he said. "But first we must drink some tea. A distant cousin sent it from Darjeeling. You can't find it anywhere else in Nazareth except in my relatives' homes. We all like this tea. It is a family well acquainted with beverage."

"What do you do to earn a living?" Melanie asked him.

"I am in the process of becoming involved in import and export. It's a difficult place for that, highly bureaucratized. Meanwhile, I am working in pest control."

"Are there roaches here?"

"It's more a country of waterbugs and multilegged hairy creatures. Very bothersome. My slogan is 'Insects Are Hazardous to Health.' It has gotten me business. Fortunate to my line, Israelis are highly conscious of cleanliness. In fact, it's a good country for employment in the pest-control field."

"So why are you switching to import-export?"

"There is only local travel involved in pest control. I would not be called to Bombay, for instance. They have their own industry, where I have learned my business. I am most interested in travel."

Cleo seemed to be staring at Nathan's calves. His body was just

36

beginning to soften, and his shirt, unbuttoned nearly to his waist, revealed that his flesh had formed small rolls, beginning there. It was easy to imagine those rolls creeping up and down his body. His face was pocked too, more like Paladin's than Richard Burton's, and yet he had the kind of self-confidence that made women feel that if he wasn't attractive to them, the fault was theirs.

"Where are you from in the States?" asked Nathan. "Did you work for Cleo over there?"

"New York," she answered. "We met in Nazareth."

"Are you an immigrant?" he asked her. "Will you stay here? Or are you simply on a brief visit?"

"She's working," said Cleo. "A journalist."

"There are too many words in the world already," he answered. "Have you ever thought about trying to do something about that? Word control, perhaps. It may be a business venture worth looking into. I'd be glad to offer advice, as consultant."

They walked through the streets of Upper Nazareth very slowly. Nathan and Cleo walked to be admired more than to see things. But Melanie was interested in looking. She saw neat windows of candies so geometrically arranged as to make them seem a mathematical exercise, hardware store windows that looked like a collage of auto parts, headless women's clothing mannequins wearing very tight sweaters and miniskirts, foreign magazine shops, cosmetic boutiques with lipsticks lined up like bullets.

"I'd like to buy a notebook," Melanie told them. "It's more authentic to write my experiences on locally produced paper, somehow."

"I do not think there is a Nazareth paper mill," said Nathan. "I am ignorant on the subject of the paper industry."

"Here's the stationery store." Cleo pointed to a shack set off from the main road by a few feet. They walked inside. Melanie looked around the shop in awe. Mounds of loose sheets of paper, notebooks, gift cards, maps, ribbons, and paper clips were randomly together in precarious stacks. Perched on top of one pile was an old radio, blaring the news. The store owner was reading a Yiddish newspaper with a magnifying glass. He didn't look up at them.

"Pardon me, kind sir," said Nathan. "Perhaps you can assist my dear friend from America."

"If she's from America, she needs a lot of help," said the old man in Yiddish.

"I'm interested in a notebook and some postcards."

"Find it, it's yours."

"What about the postcards? Aren't they separate?"

"Do I look like a man who discriminates?" But he did go away to the back of the store, coming back with a shoe box that looked like one of the first.

"Do you speak French?" he said. *"Voilà!"* He placed his box in front of Melanie. She saw dusty photographs, bent and dog-eared, of ancient sites. "Don't you have something a little more modern?"

"You want the Empire State Building?" he said.

"She would like something to be used for mailing purposes."

"You put a stamp on it, it goes," said the man.

"I will just take a notebook."

"Only one? You have nothing to say?"

"Two," she told him.

"Three," said the man. "I know my customers."

Six

"What about sex?" Agram asked Melanie the next morning. They met for breakfast in the same café. Cleo was helping to cater a wedding in Haifa. "Do you like it?"

"Pardon me?" she replied. "I would rather discuss your day in Jerusalem."

"Jerusalem," he said. "Have you been there? It is the most beautiful city in the world. I will take you. I have many friends in Jerusalem."

"What do you do when you go there?"

"Why do you want to know?"

"I want to understand who you are."

"Not now," he said. "So what about sex? Did your husband make you happy?"

"I suppose so," said Melanie. "I don't have a lot of basis for comparison."

"A beautiful girl like you," he said. "Why not?"

"It's an uncomfortable subject for me," she said. "I don't quite know how to discuss it, to describe my past, or how I feel about it. In fact, I'm not so sure I want to. After all, I hardly know you."

"Practice," said Agram. "Say what you know. I will help you. You see this," he said. He pulled out a necklace from his back pocket, a long chain with a clump of gold and silver initials dangling from it. "The girls gave them to me to remember. The *E* is diamonds. It's called pavé. The girl was Eva, a Hungarian on Easter vacation. In America you have something called testimony. A woman says she likes the soap so everyone else can know to use it. We have the same here. A pretty girl says in the newspaper that something makes her pretty. The others want it too.''

"How did you meet them all?''

"I sit,'' said Agram. "They come to me like you did. They are looking for something, and I am here, waiting for them. They have been coming to Nazareth for years now.''

"And are they interchangeable for you? Are all of the experiences exactly the same? Or do they seem separate and different? I would guess that after a while the women would merge into each other, that you can't tell them apart too clearly. You might even forget their names.''

"No, no,'' said Agram. "They are all very different for me. I love them. It is possible to love many times. And why not?''

"Don't they get in each other's way? Doesn't each woman hope that she'll be the one you love the most, that she'll cause you to stop with all the others and spend your life only with her? And what about your wife? How does she understand it? What does she think about your spending so much time with other women?''

"Difficult questions,'' said Agram. "I married my wife for the sake of my mother. My mother said I must have a wife. She is dead now, but she was a religious Moslem who ruled our house. My mother was the boss. She was always right. The whole family asked her for help. Once, when a cousin was engaged through an arrangement, she came to my mother upset, claiming that the man she was to marry didn't smell good. The cousin was unhappy. No one else knew what to do, so they sent the girl to my mother. I was young, but I remember them whispering in the kitchen. My mother asked if he took a bath on Fridays. The cousin didn't know. My mother said she would talk to the man herself. The next day he came to our kitchen and I heard them whispering. My mother gave him a bottle of perfume from Egypt. She told him if he wanted to make my cousin happy he had to go to the hot springs in Tiberias at least twice in a week, then cover himself with perfume. The man agreed. They are still happy together. They have many children.''

"What about your own wife? How does she feel about the way you live?"

"My wife doesn't ask questions; she takes care of me and the children, and her mother and our house. She is very busy."

"Do you love her?"

"She's a good woman," said Agram. "But she doesn't understand."

"All husbands like to think that," said Melanie. "It's their way of making themselves desirable. You want me to believe that maybe I will have the comprehension that others don't, that you will then love me for it."

"It is all very possible," said Agram. "Life is very funny," he said.

"Let me think it over," Melanie replied. "I'm not the spontaneous sort of person."

"Take your time," said Agram. "You can tell me tomorrow."

That afternoon, Melanie walked through town, wandering in and out of shops to get a sense of what it was like there. Around four, she found a chocolate store a little off the main road. Someone had taped a hand-lettered sign in English in the store window: *Orange Peels from Chocolate Made by Hands*. This drew her inside. "What are those orange peels exactly?" she asked the man behind the counter.

"Please," answered a customer standing near her, a tall, graceful soldier holding a bag that seemed much too small for him to carry. He motioned for her to try them. "They are not made by machine, the way you do everything in America," he said.

"I would like a small bag," she told the shopkeeper.

"Not so small," said the stranger. "I will buy them." He ordered a kilo in melodic English which sounded somehow childlike, because he was nearly whispering. "They are very good. My name is Mordecai Ben-Samech."

"I am Melanie Markowitz," she said. "How do you do."

"Yes, how do you do." He imitated the tone of her phrase.

He held her bag with his, and they walked out of the store together. He walked quickly, almost gently, leading her to a café next door to the shop. Not the place where she sat with Agram and Cleo, but another, hidden from Agram's vision. *"Nu,* so tell me," he said patiently, kindly. "I have been wondering who you are."

"What do you mean? We have never met before."

"Meeting and seeing are different," he said. "I see you talking with Agram and the American woman."

"Do you work for the police?"

"Not exactly," he said. "This is a country in a war. We are careful."

"But who could I possibly be?" she asked.

"It doesn't matter. I ask for myself, and not for my government."

"I am an American."

"That you tell me," said Mordecai, perturbed. "Do you think I don't know that already? Tell me something else."

"I'm a journalist writing an article about the Arabs."

"You can't write about your own people?"

"Who are my people?"

"You are not a Zionist?"

"I'm not sure that's relevant."

"Are you married?"

"No, are you?"

He smiled then. "It's not so simple." Like Agram, he looked down at his watch at regular intervals. He had a six-inch watchband in black leather, sprinkled with metal studs. It was frightening to look at, unexpected on his arm. His hands were big, with large fingers more muscular than fleshy. He wore glasses, tinted brown, so his eyes were hidden. His hair was short and clean, cut in place. It looked immovable. His nose was too small, really pug, unexpected on so broad a face. His lips were his strangest feature, two shades darker than the rest of his face. They were a deep red, in two points on the top and the sides, not in the manner of Clara Bow, but more like a bird's, bent on the task of eating all the other birds' seed. Through these tightly defined lips came a soft voice, asking questions. He made seduction seem inevitable, with a look in his eyes that alluded to future victories.

"So you are not married?" he repeated.

"Does that surprise you?"

"You are telling the truth?"

"I was married once, for a few years."

"Aha," he said. "How did I know?"

"You just guessed."

"I could feel it," said Mordecai. "I know people. Just like that."
He snapped his fingers, then looked at her with the expression of a
conqueror. Melanie looked back at him, puzzled.

"Why did you buy me those orange peels?"

"You mean your husband did not buy you candy?"

"You are not my husband." She laughed.

"I want to show you Israel," he answered. "Not the Israel of this
very small town, but the other Israel, with villas and horses. The *real*
Israel. It's a beautiful country. Maybe you will write about that for
America."

"We know a lot about Israel," she answered. "It's the Israeli
Arabs we don't know too much about."

"Maybe there's a reason," he replied.

"What could that reason be?"

"You think you should know everything?"

"Only enough to understand."

"If I tell you about them, you cannot understand," he said. "Life
isn't easy here."

"Can you recommend any good books on the subject, or libraries I
could visit for background information?"

"A book is just a book," said Mordecai. "You need someone to
show you. You are very fortunate that we met."

"And what about you?" asked Melanie, flirtatious.

"Not bad," he told her smiling, making *bad* sound more like *bed*
when he said it. "I like you American girls."

"Have you known many?"

"Don't ask," said Mordecai. "Better you don't know. It's too
soon for that."

"I'm interested," she said. "I want to know what happened to
other American women here."

"They all fell in love," said Mordecai, laughing. "It is a romantic

43

place. So will you." He smiled at her again, but this time she couldn't quite read the intention of his smile.

"Were you born here?"

"I was born on Kibbutz Malka on the Sea of Galilee. When I was fifteen, I was the national champion for swimming across the sea against four hundred others."

"Where did your family come from?"

"Morocco," said Mordecai. "My parents came together to kibbutz. My mother lives there still. I am in Haifa."

"Do your friends call you Mordecai?"

"Motke."

"Like Morty?" she asked him.

"A mistake the Americans always are making," he answered.

"Do you find us all similar?"

"You are asking me to say if I like you?"

"Can you know the answer already?"

"Of course I can know. It's my business. Don't ask so many questions." He smiled at her again, in a way that clearly showed he liked her. She smiled back at him, and the color rushed to her face very quickly, making her pretty.

"Where do you stay here?" he asked.

"With Fuad and Shari Hassan."

"She married him in America," said Mordecai. "Do they give you a room by yourself?"

"Sort of. It's a small place."

"Would you like to stay in Tiberias? I have another apartment there," he added.

"I don't think so. I like being with Shari and Fuad."

"Why with them? There are three million other people here."

"My piece is about Arabs, and besides, I knew Shari from America."

"But why are you writing about Arabs?" he asked. "Is anyone interested? Do they want to know that in America?"

"The readers of my paper want to know."

"Are they important people?" he asked. "Can they change things?"

44

"Do you know who can change things?"

"So why do you write for them?"

"I believe in the paper. We are providing a service."

"Maybe it is just for yourself," he said. "Maybe it is only you who thinks it is important."

"Do you do something more important? Can you change things?"

"More than you," he said confidently. "I don't work for a few."

"Who employs you?"

"The government. I am in the army in security. Nazareth is my place. I see what happens here."

"Can you tell me?"

"*Chic-chak?*" he said. "Just like that one two you want answers? You want me to say everything now? I will tell you something tomorrow when we are eating."

"You never invited me."

"Americans are too polite." He laughed. "Please, will you eat some dinner?"

"I always eat dinner."

"You understand me, so why do you do this?"

"Because I want to be properly invited."

"The Queen from England," said Mordecai. "I will come to you at seven."

Melanie shook Mordecai's hand. "Nice to meet you," she said.

"You are funny," he answered.

Seven

"If only I could find a place for myself here," Shari said to Melanie.
"Some friends maybe or a community where I felt as though I
belonged. Life wouldn't be half so difficult then. But I don't really fit
here, and I'm not sure I ever will. Even at the cooperative nursery
school, the other teachers seem suspicious. They never invite me to
visit their families or ask me to tell them about my life. I feel as
though they distrust me for living here. It's as if they wonder why I'd
come here if I had a choice to live in America instead. I know I left
America as much to get away as to live with Fuad. But I do love him.
He's an interesting man, far more complex than the boys I knew in
school, who just seemed to care about being lawyers or doctors or
playing basketball. Fuad has an ideal, something he really believes. I
never met a man who believed in anything before Fuad. He's serious
about the novel, though I don't know that he'll ever really finish it."

"What's it about?" Melanie asked. "He doesn't seem to talk
about it much."

"Act surprised if he tells you. Not that it's a secret. He's been
working on it for years. It's about a Palestinian who lives under
occupation, and the daily humiliations that make up his life. He falls
in love with a progressive Swedish doctor who is working in the Old
City of Jerusalem. She talks him into leaving Palestine to live with
her in Stockholm. He marries her, and they move to Sweden, where
he earns his living selling Bedouin antiquities. But the Swedes, a
cut-and-dried sort of people, don't understand the ornate dresses and

47

mirrors and beads that he carries. He feels alienated and alone, and worse than that, he feels useless. The Swedes act cold to him, and he longs to return. They have a baby, a boy that he loves very much. His unhappiness increases, though, and his wife finally agrees to try living in Jerusalem again. She gets a job as a doctor at Hadassah Hospital, but the other doctors are wary of her, and she feels awkward there. The child develops problems. They try to send him to a school, but he can't seem to learn to speak Arabic. Finally, the wife leaves, taking the child with her. He then marries a girl from his village, an arranged marriage, really. But the girl is far too simple, too devoted to him for his liking. He gives her books about feminism, about independence, about life in other countries, but she doesn't understand. He feels hopelessly trapped.''

"It sounds like a wonderful book," said Melanie. "But is life really so difficult here? Does Fuad feel that same kind of conflict?"

"It's hard for both of us. Actually, we would belong in America much more easily. In an academic community or even a big city somewhere.''

"So why not go back?"

"Because he believes in fighting and feels that if the struggle is properly waged, the rewards will be worth the pain. He says that to leave would be to give in. He sees leaving as desertion. Besides, Nazareth is his life. All of Fuad's hopes are based on his sense that justice can be won.''

"But does he understand what justice really means, how odd and whimsical history is with right and wrong?''

"He thinks it's not limited to a few; he's prepared to fight for it if he must. In fact, this idea of justice is the basis for his own confusion. He can't accept what's happening now.''

"Will he fight, do you think?"

"I don't know. It's impossible to say what will happen.''

"How do you feel about the Palestinians?"

"I can see right and wrong on both sides," said Shari. "It's impossible not to.''

"Does it make you angry, or bitter?"

"No," said Shari. "Sad more than anything. I don't understand how any resolution can take place that will be satisfying to more than a few."

"Do you think the rest of the world is any different?"

"Probably not," said Shari. "But I don't live in the rest of the world."

"Do you know a man named Mordecai Ben-Samech?" Melanie asked. "It's funny how little first names mean to me here. I don't have a context for understanding them. The name Peggy has an image for me. So does Sharon, or Michael. But not Mordecai. The most I can come up with is a child in a cotton beard acting in a Purim play."

"It's a very common name here."

"I met him in the candy store, the one that's off the main road. He bought me a bag of orange peels."

"When Fuad and I first met," said Shari, "he would bring me salted chick peas in a small paper bag. Who knows where he ever found them in Ann Arbor."

"Mordecai's invited me to dinner tonight."

"You know Fuad's mother will be suspicious," said Shari. They both were suddenly aware of Fuad's mother, leaving her room and padding softly nearby. Shari gave Melanie a look of warning.

"What is her name?" asked Melanie, pointing. "I can't call her Fuad's mother forever."

"It's how she wants to be known," answered Shari. "They say *um* Fuad in Arabic."

"Why would she be suspicious?"

"In many parts of the world it's assumed that all foreigners, especially newspaper reporters, are spies on the payroll of their governments. I never knew that until I came here."

"Who could I possibly be spying for? Wouldn't they have sent someone with more knowledge of the area than I have? Older and with more experience?"

"Not necessarily," Shari said. "If they did, though, they'd probably advise her to feign ignorance."

"Who could I be working for?" Melanie asked.

"There are a lot of choices. The Israelis themselves, or the CIA, or the Russians, or even the Chinese. Or maybe you could work for a militant Palestinian group, trying to infiltrate the center. Even my parents could have sent you, offering money in exchange for a report on our lives. I wouldn't put it past them. You'd be surprised how many people have good reasons to want information about other people's lives.''

Fuad's mother entered then, bringing her ever-present tray with small glasses of tea balanced carefully on top of it. Each glass had a clump of green leaves in its center. ''That's mint,'' said Shari, seeing Melanie looking. Fuad's mother said something to Shari in Arabic. She spoke quickly.

''She wants to know if you are married.''

''No.''

Fuad's mother didn't look at Melanie while she asked, but directed the questions to Shari as though she were the subject in question. When Melanie answered, she showed no reaction. ''I am divorced,'' said Melanie. ''Bad luck. But I'm looking,'' she smiled. ''I would marry again. The first time was just a mistake. We were too young.''

''She says that no one is too young,'' said Shari.

''Be careful from Agram,'' said Fuad's mother to Melanie in English. She looked her in the eyes and repeated the sentence.

''Be careful of Agram,'' Shari corrected.

''Why?''

''He has a family,'' said Fuad's mother. ''He isn't nice.''

''What should I call you?''

''I am Fuad's mother,'' she replied. '' 'Fuad's mother' is good,'' she said.

''OK. Fuad's mother.'' Melanie smiled at her. ''I don't really understand, though, why I should be careful. Can he do something to me?''

''He is famous,'' said Fuad's mother.

''I am old enough to take care of myself.''

''No,'' said Fuad's mother in a voice that sounded surprisingly strong and young. ''No,'' she repeated again. Then she padded away.

50

Later that evening, Melanie wrote to her editor, William Hall, about how she felt in Nazareth.

Lower Nazareth, where the Arabs live, is the city of gospel. In that sense it's atypical, because there are as many Christian Arabs as Moslems here. There are ten or so places where Jesus was conceived, all marked by rocks and fences and three-language placards. Many of the boy children in the town are named Jesus (Issa in Arabic) or Muhammad. Like other famous sites, Lower Nazareth has seen the influence of Walt Disney. There are replica souvenirs of famous Bible moments, as well as postcards with arrows pointing to holy stones and watering holes. Early Beatles music seems to be playing here often, and American show tunes. *Porgy and Bess* and *West Side Story* are both very popular. That and a heartbreaking, wailing woman singer named Um Kul Suum. People seem to love music.

The heat has a profound effect. It compounds the heaviness of living somewhere ancient. Other hot countries are different. The Caribbean, for instance, is just as hot but it's lazy, not frenetic, with slow-moving breezes and days that are long stretches beginning after the morning is already over, short days that end in the early evenings at sunset with steel drums and a drink.

Time passes slowly. The days can feel endless, because the heat seems to lengthen them. And waking up warm is too much connected to the night before, not enough of a beginning or an ending, but a wearying way of linking evenings and mornings together. Even so, when I think of the days I've spent here, they've seemed rapid-fire, as if I am having a series of short and powerful dreams.

Even the Catholics, all in light blue with Holy Mother of Mary charms on their watches, even they have to respond to these frenetic surroundings, if only to complain in loud voices that there's urine in the streets, that their pale skins are turning red despite their efforts to maintain the whiteness. So much of the world is treated by them as if it were just a pretty girl, the same pleasant yet incidental part of life as a breeze on a summer day. Diverting, but not to be taken very seriously.

It's a place where serious intellectuals hide in dark rooms, where candy store owners write poems: they are all so serious, they are paralyzed with their knowledge of the world and its misdeeds. Nazareth is unforgettable: hills and a moon that's strange the first time you see it because it's so close and approachable, not as far away as the moon seemed to be in the past.

I've met many Arabs, men especially, who have been to America. The women are hidden. They are rarely in cafes, or out at night. Hassan is typical. Intelligent and enterprising, he went to the U.S. to study air condi-

51

tioning. He wanted to change the impossible summers. I met him at his father's souvenir shop, where he now works. Though he returned well versed in air-conditioning procedures, he couldn't find anywhere that would agree to let him try. "We need something to complain about every summer," he was told any time he broached the subject. So he's working in his father's store, waiting for the climate to change. Of course, he could work for Israelis, who seem all in favor of cold air no matter who achieves it. The only problem is that he went to the U.S. to learn to make things better for his own people. He told me when we met that air conditioning is his profession, and heating is his hobby.

I have seen very few American women living among Arabs. The culture seems very different from our own. For single people especially, life among the Arabs, without a family, seems especially hard. It really is a family-oriented place. Single women are suspect. Upper Nazareth, which is Israeli, is a little different. It's a more Western place in general, with a shopping mall, and smartly dressed women.

Even so, Upper Nazareth isn't quite a Western place. The people work slowly. I thought it was because of the heat at first, but now I'm not sure of the reason.

Israeli soldiers are everywhere. They often seem to be watching each other. In the fifties, we saw posters of Equal Israelis in the army, men and women fighting side by side, smiling with fervent nonsexist dedication. Yet it's the men who are the clear masters. They are the soldiers, and soldiers in Israel are kings. Women, most of them anyway, even the professionals, seem to want to be beauty queens, movie stars, or, at the very least, photographer's models. They are beautiful women, with unusual skin and hair.

Some claim the sex roles are so classic because of the war. Male soldiers are inordinately elevated. Women go into the army, too, but they seem to do menial jobs there, typing and filing, or teaching young children. They don't fight, or do anything where power and authority are involved.

Sex roles are very traditional. That is something I hadn't expected, assuming somehow the socialist ideal from Russia. In fact, the character of the country has little to do with eastern Europe. It's a Sephardic place, with nothing in common with American Judaism. I expected a bagels-and-lox society, and though I've seen an occasional bagel on a vendor's cart in Tel Aviv, I've never seen lox, or cream cheese.

My impressions might change a thousand times in my time here, but now I find this an unusually complex place, full of contradictions and surprises. One of the first things I noticed right away was how oblivious I was, the first time through here, to any life going on around me, how easy it was to accept the statues and monuments and places we visited on tour as being all that there was. Of course, life for the people who live here is the same as it is anywhere else—problems, big and small, seem to occupy most of everyone's day, and circumstances are difficult for the average person. The East and the West coexist here, not all that peacefully but in a way that is still in the process of evolving.

One thing is important to tell you about Nazareth old and new: it is beautiful. Not the passing beauty of a young girl filled with hope and promise, but the overwhelming beauty of that which is eternal and profound, as the ocean can be, or a foreign sunrise. From every angle, the city is overwhelming. It's hills and a valley, winding into and out of itself. Even the sky seems more open, more three-dimensional than any sky I've ever seen. The stars are distinct and clear. They almost seem close.

About what the Arabs think: I hate to say this, but I am already beginning to have my doubts about being able to write anything that is both fair and broadly representative. I've met some Arabs, but they seem to be very different from each other. One in particular, named Agram, reminds me of Marlon Brando. I'm not quite sure why (did Brando have a wandering eye in any of his films?), though I know Agram has seen *The Godfather* enough to memorize the lines. I'm sure my feelings here will evolve, but at this point I can't predict the outcome.

I've met few Israelis, though a man named Mordecai, a soldier, is taking me to dinner tonight. He will introduce me to his friends, I hope. I've also met a Jewish Indian, a Don Juan type who doesn't seem typical of much.

I will try to write you every ten days, so you will have concrete proof that I am well, watching, and still in Nazareth.

Melanie

Eight

He arrived at seven. He rapped on the door loudly, as if he were completing an important military rescue mission and had no time for niceties. "I'll get it," said Shari to Melanie. "I'm curious." *"Shalom,"* said Mordecai. "I'm Mordecai Ben-Samech. I am happy to meet you."

"Hello," said Shari, stretching her right hand out to shake his. "I am Shari Kliger."

"I know," he said. "I am looking for the journalist from America."

"You must mean my friend in the other room."

"Is it Shari like the song?" he asked her.

"What song?"

" 'Sherry Baby,' " he said. "It was popular in America. A girl sent it to me many years ago. It is on a small black record. The Four Seasons are the singers. They are very famous over there. You don't know them? I think they are almost as famous as Cliff Richards."

"Who is Cliff Richards?" asked Shari.

"Are you sure you are an American?"

"Excuse me," she said and went to get Melanie, who was listening from the kitchen. "Not bad," said Shari. "I've seen worse."

Melanie walked into the living room slowly, awkwardly, conscious of Fuad's mother padding back and forth around her. Melanie's knees seemed to buckle underneath her as she walked, and her hands felt clammy. She had tried to look her best, though. Her hair, normally hanging limply on the side of her face, was tied back with a bright red ribbon she'd bought in the market, and she wore Mexican silver hoops in her ears, large, shiny circles that swung back and forth with some grace. They added an occasional glint to her cheeks. She had lined her eyes in dark brown pencil, and this made them more intense.

"You are very nice," said Mordecai. Melanie's legs straightened when he said that. Mordecai seemed to be all glasses at first. They were tinted a dark pink, nearly opaque. His eyes hid behind them. He looked clean and strong and competent. He wore a yellow shirt, very pale, not oxford cloth or drip-dry, but something in between. He was naked beneath it, and the shirt was mostly unbuttoned. He was hairy: not overly so but nicely hairy; his chest looked tufted under his shirt.

"So," he said. "Well."

"So, well," she replied. They smiled at each other. He looked taller than she'd remembered, more than six feet.

"We are going now. You won't be sorry." His arms swung forward, as if that very gesture could carry them both away. His arms appeared ready to encircle even the largest subject of his whim. He seemed to burst with energy. Melanie followed him, not very far behind. "You are going slowly for a reason," he said as he went bounding out the door and then into his car. "I thought you Americans were in a rush."

He opened the door for her from inside. He was the commanding general, she a favored soldier entitled to ride by his side. What would happen seemed up to him. The car, a Mediterranean version of a wooden-sided station wagon, was white—not the whitewashed white of Mykonos or Sani-White—more the dusty cream that passes for white in glaring sunshine. A once white, mottled so carefully by too-warm days and soot that the innocent observer could easily be tricked. The car was the shape of a streamlined ambulance, a little closer to the ground than that, with enclosed walls instead of windows. The only windows were in front, one on each side. The most unusual characteristics of the car were two things Mordecai had added. One was hanging dice, bright green sponges with black bits of

56

felt for dots. The other was a large gun across the floor in front. The dice were held to the mirror by a shoestring.

As for the gun, it was an unusually large and thin weapon. "You're looking at the Uzi," said Mordecai. The word sounded more like chocolate candy filled with caramel cream than the name of a gun.

They drove off in his car, and it seemed at first as if they were driving away forever. His arm rested very easily on her nervous shoulder. His head was held high, glasses perfectly balanced, nose facing the setting sun. He didn't say too much. "Where are we going?" she asked.

"Leave it to Beaver," he answered. Then he turned on the radio. A woman who sounded like a Girl Scout troop leader said a few words in rapid-fire Hebrew, then burst into song. It was a marching song, frisky and optimistic.

"What's the song about?" she asked him.

"It's about tomorrow," he said. He smiled at her. She smiled back, saying, "By then, I'll know where we're going."

"Patience," he said. "It's a surprise. You will like it. I know you." Then he looked over at her with an expression that told her he didn't really know her, but was only guessing. "Trust me," he said.

"Do I have a choice?"

They pulled up in front of something that looked like a split-level ranch house, on a hilltop above the Sea of Galilee. A large neon sign, discordant in the ancient skies, proclaimed, *Ranch*. The *Ranch* blinked on and off. "What is this?" asked Melanie.

"You can't read?" he answered. "Did you go to college?"

"Yes," she said. "I understand the term. But what does it stand for?"

"It's a ranch," said Mordecai. "A ranch is a ranch. You didn't think we had them, did you?"

"What do you do on the ranch?"

"We eat," said Mordecai. "We eat steak, like America. What do you think, we don't know how to live? Nazareth is not the real Israel."

57

"Is the ranch?"

"Maybe the same as Nazareth," said Mordecai. "It's not an easy place to understand."

"You can say that again," Melanie answered.

And he did.

The inside of the restaurant was a replica of a Kansas City steakhouse: there was sawdust on the floor, framed photographs of cowboys with lassos and big grins, and a waitress dressed in buckeye fringe. She walked to the table with the gait of a drum majorette, bending her knees upward to the Tammy Wynette song on the speakers. "How ya doin', Tex?" she said to Mordecai with a southwestern twang.

"Mordecai," he said. "Call me Motke. Where's Big Bob?" He pronounced *Bob* as if it were a word with five or six *B*'s.

"Howdy, Mordy," shouted a voice from the kitchen. Then Bob burst through the swinging half-doors, saloon doors really, that separated the kitchen from the dining room. They were more like shutters hung halfway down. He had a steel hook instead of a right hand. "Who's the little lady?" he shouted, waving the hook in Melanie's direction.

"Meet my friend from America," said Mordecai.

"Howdy, miss," said Big Bob. "What do you call yourself?"

"Melanie Markowitz."

"What are you doing in these parts?"

"I might ask the same of you."

"I'm in the restaurant business," said Bob. "This here is proof of the pudding."

"He was in Vietnam," said Mordecai. "An American hero."

"What part of America are you from?" asked Melanie.

"Born in Youngstown, Ohio, but we moved to Dallas when I was young," said Bob. "My father was restless. I'm the real thing, all right."

"So what are you doing in Israel?"

"It's John Wayne country," said Bob. "The men are men and the ladies are pretty. I hope you don't mind my saying that. I know you girls have different ideas, these days. I came straight from Nam," he said. "Met some Israelis over in Bangkok, and they offered me this piece of property. Have some steak," he continued. "You'll feel better. I'll bet it's been a long time since you've had a piece of meat like this. Not since back home."

"Where does it come from?"

"Right here," said Bob. "We've got cows and all the rest of it. Enjoy your meal, little lady. Anything you'd like to hear on the juke?"

"Otis Redding," said Melanie. "It doesn't matter what."

"Otis Redding it is," said Big Bob. "The guest is the chief on this ranch. Enjoy your meal. As they say over here, *l' chayim.*" He raised his hook to the heavens.

"You too," said Melanie. Bob waved his good hand in farewell and walked toward the kitchen, slamming his way through the slotted half-doors with force.

"Don't they say *l' chayim* in America?" Mordecai asked. "What would you like to eat? You heard him. They have *steakim.*"

"Does that mean little steaks?"

"Why little? They're big like Texas. It means more than one. You can have three if you want them."

"I couldn't possibly eat three."

"No problem," said Mordecai. "I will order for you and for me. When the food comes, we will talk." He smiled at her with great self-assurance.

The waitress brought the steaks then, big slabs of meat on large metal trays. "You see," said Mordecai. "Big like Texas."

"How am I going to be able to eat that?"

"You just begin," he said. "Slowly, slowly. You'll learn. It takes time to be an Israeli, but you can do it. We have time. Watch me," he said. Then he cut a bite-sized piece off the edge of the steak, a small and perfect cube, and inserted it into his mouth very carefully. He chewed with great care.

"I know how to eat a steak," she told him.

"So what are you waiting?" he asked her.

Nine

Agram and Cleo were having troubles. Cleo told Melanie about it late one afternoon when they ran into each other shopping. Both women were buying plastics. They surveyed the shops together, marveling at their choices: not just the predictable plastic things like garbage pails or dish drainers, but everything else: shoes from China and crates for carrying eggs as well as dressy evening bags in woven plastic gold. The plastics all came in a wide range of colors—greens, reds, yellows, blues, even silver, a dull gunmetal.

Cleo bought a bright blue rubber mat for the shower. "I change my bathroom color scheme every three months," she said. "At least, I buy a new something for it. They don't have shower curtains here, so I have to rely on the floor for variety, more than I would at home." Melanie purchased a lime-green bucket. "They seem to use buckets for everything, so I thought I'd try one," she said. "The houses all have half a dozen. I can at least do my wash in this, and carry home souvenirs in it."

"I don't know if I should really discuss this with you," Cleo began when they sat down for coffee. "But you're an outsider and it's easier. Agram and I are having problems." As usual, Cleo looked wonderful: Balinese. She was swathed in a batik sarong of dark purple and green. "What beautiful colors," said Melanie.

"They're from rare Indonesian berries, found only near Hindu sun temples," said Cleo. Around her right ankle she'd tied a red polka-dot ribbon, Cleo's addition. The nails on both her hands and feet were done in elaborate designs: plum with small flowers painted in white at the tip of each.

Melanie wore a navy blue turtleneck sweater, even though it was hot, and a small flowered A-line skirt. She'd gotten perfume at a cosmetics shop the day before, White Nile, and she had sparingly dabbed it on all her pulse points. Even so she could smell it as she moved. Maybe the perfume had been what she was missing, though she feared it might be the very scent they sold to tourists by the carload. They'd had something called Empire State Building that she felt was probably more popular with the locals, but it smelled too sweet. The bottle was nice, though. Maybe she could buy one for a souvenir. White Nile was musky, not her usual summer floral for special occasions, but something more real, dark and earthy. On her ears were the long coins, and a thin gold-colored bracelet fell gracefully over her wrist.

"You're wearing perfume," said Cleo. "And bigger earrings. You seem to be changing here. Is it the place or something else?"

"I'm trying," said Melanie. "I haven't been exposed to much that was different. I suppose I've led a very sheltered life."

"Have you traveled much?"

"Only guidebook kinds of trips. This is my first experience living in a foreign country. I find myself watching carefully, anxious for things to happen to me, happy when they do. It's as if I came here to experience life in a way that I couldn't at home."

"Weren't you able to make things happen there?"

"I was," said Melanie. "But they were predictable things. I married another student and got a job on a small paper. Our life hummed along, but there were no real highs or lows. Except, of course, when we got our divorce."

"Why did that happen?"

"Maybe because we competed too intensely with each other. We made life harder instead of easier. We were each other's toughest critic. That got in the way of our ever being able to feel any kind of ease or trust. I still love him even now."

"Would you marry each other again?"

"It's too late," she said. "We've hurt each other too seriously by now. We'd have to be more complacent about the past, maybe have more distance from it. We are both unforgiving, angry that things didn't work out better. Besides, we were young and didn't know enough about what to expect. Neither of us really knew how good what we had was."

"That's part of my problem with Agram," said Cleo. "He doesn't realize that the reason he's attracted to me is because I am a woman of broad experience. He admires that experience, having had numerous encounters of his own. Even so, because he found out about Nathan, he is angry with me. I told him that Nathan is just a companion. His voice is soothing and he helps me to fall asleep. I'm not in love with Nathan at all. But I don't like being alone at night. Agram doesn't either. He often goes home to his wife. I tried to equate his cigar box with Nathan, telling him that those letters are much worse than a pleasant and harmless companion. He denied that, saying the women are far away. 'It's me and no one, or nothing,' he told me. I asked where his wife fit into all this, but he claimed that his wife was not the issue. Now what?" Cleo looked desperate. "Of course I love him. I love him more than any man I've ever known."

"Maybe that's because you can't marry him," said Melanie. "It could be that is why he's all the more desirable. And maybe Nathan's close range makes him easier to dismiss."

"I don't care about reasons," said Cleo. "I want to be with Agram no matter what. Will you talk to him for me? I know he likes you. He thinks you're smart."

"What can I say?"

"Just explain things," said Cleo. "Isn't that the normal job of a journalist? It should be easy, especially now that you know all the facts."

So Melanie agreed. Even if she couldn't help Cleo, she could at least see Agram again. Early the next morning, she found him sitting as usual. He seemed to her to look even bigger sitting than when he was standing up. Not actually bigger but stronger of presence, the kingly type who turned any chair where he deigned to sit into a throne. Agram made you feel his physical strength. To see him holding court in the middle of the day was to force you into responding: you either had to be part of his session or avoid it at all costs. There was no middle ground. Even those who weren't used to reacting did to him: Idaho tourists turned around to steal another look at what he was doing, and who was sitting there with him. They'd turn away so fast it seemed they'd felt something unexpected, something they didn't know and weren't sure they wanted to learn. That something was just the strength of his presence.

Melanie was attracted to him. She tried to understand why, and realized that there's something to being around a person who thinks he has all the answers. Even so, she knew perfectly well he had no sense of humor. This seemed to her to be a sad truth of powerful men all over the world. Agram did consider himself witty, however. He would say a sentence, anything really, then smile the same wry smile as someone who has made an amusing remark. "Nice day," he'd say. He would look as though this were the cleverest possible statement, or as if he had made reference to something sexual that only he were capable of knowing. That aside, it was easy to understand why Cleo loved him.

There's something about a very big man. Poems have been written, songs sung, pictures painted of women who are large and appealing, but no one has ever done the same for the broad, strong man. Many spend years with them, for good reason. Fathers are never big enough. Mothers are, even the fragile sparrow types. Agram's size alone accounted for some of his charisma.

Melanie approached him with the uneasy calm of knowing she had to bring up an unpleasant matter.

"Miss America," he said as usual, whispering suggestively. "Five cents U.S. for what you are thinking."

"Nothing much," she answered, not wanting to give away her mission at once.

"You can't fool me," he said. "I am an expert in human beings."

"I've been thinking about how hard Nazareth is to understand."

"What especially? Just ask me. I'll tell you the answers. My family has been here for generations."

"What do the people really want here?"

"The same thing they want anywhere else. A good life."

"But what would make their lives good? It's different in every society, isn't it?"

"People are the same all over," he said with great assurance. "You and I aren't as different as we look. We eat three times each day, and have a roof when we sleep."

"But isn't there a difference in the kind of roof, the kind of food, and what happens between mealtimes? Isn't the quality of life a very personal thing, something that varies a lot from place to place?"

"Yes and no," he said. "We all want to be happy. We want a country, a family, a nice house, a good job. Enough money."

"It seems to me those wants take many forms," she told him.

"In America, you learn it is not polite to say, 'I want.' Here, we say it all the time. That's why we can get the small things, but not the big ones."

"What's the difference?"

"A small thing is a good meal, cooked in the home. All Palestinians have this. So do most people in the Arab world, except the Israelis. The Israelis have a state. A state is a big want. If they spent all their time cooking meals, they might not have a state. They have technology, and schools, and sewers, and complicated toilets, and color television. The rest of the Middle East, except for the very rich, don't have this. Israelis don't eat well—only cucumbers and our food made poorly, but they have other things that are bigger, more important."

When he said this, his lips barely moved, his manner was absolute. "Stick to me," he said. "That way, you'll know what is going on."

"What about you and Cleo?"

"A big story, that Cleo," he said. "She's a wonderful girl. She can do anything. She probably didn't tell you, but she knows how to make chocolates with her hands. She cooks better Arabic meals than many relatives. She learns fast. She's something else."

"Do you love her?"

"Love," he said. "We don't know what this is. We understand the gods better than love. Of course I love her. Why not?"

"If you love her, why do you try to change the way she is?"

"Because she doesn't make me happy. She is seeing a young nothing Indian."

"If she saw a better man, would that be easier for you?"

"No," he said. "Easy isn't the question. The question is, why is she doing this to me? Women can be very cruel. I don't want to play the second fiddle."

"What about your wife?"

"My wife has nothing to do."

"What do you mean?"

"That's another thing," he said. "My wife is my wife, and that's it. Husbands and wives are something separate. Like an arm or a leg. They are there for a reason. Sometimes because of the errors of our ancestors. Sometimes because of the laws of the universe. Cleo is another problem. She has had her husbands. I have my wife. So what? We are like a husband and a wife without the problems. Besides, men and women are different that way," he said.

"Why is that?"

"Men want a lot of wives, and they can be good to all of them. But women can only be good to one man at a time. This is history," he exclaimed.

"I find that a primitive and unreasonable way of thinking," said Melanie. "Also unbearably sexist. We are conditioned differently, but our instincts are the same."

"Look at the world," he said, moving his hand in a broad gesture in front of them. "Where do you see women with many husbands? Where? Tell me one place."

"But Cleo had four," said Melanie. "Does it matter that she didn't have them at once?"

"Of course," he said. "At once is impossible. You are still very young. You have enough time to learn everything."

She felt confused. Should she argue more for what she believed, or just accept him as he was and watch what happened? She decided the second was easier. Besides, she was in Nazareth to understand things, not change them.

"The movie *2001* is playing in Haifa," he said. "I have only seen it twice. It's really something. I love the colors. Do you want to go at

66

three o'clock? Bobby can bring us. Maybe Bobby would like to see it again too. Last time he fell asleep and had to ask me what happened."

"A good idea. It would be a nice change to see a movie."

"We have two in Nazareth. But they are mostly spaghetti cowboys. Italians with a gun. They're not bad, but they're not the same as American. Have you seen *2001* before now?"

"Yes," she said. "I've seen a few films by the director, Stanley Kubrick. One called *Dr. Strangelove.*"

"Is it bloody?" said Agram.

"Sort of. He goes crazy with power."

"Doctors are crazy people. You have to be a little crazy to go to school so long. Bobby's cousin does it. You should see him. A real casket case."

"Casket?"

"You know. A box they use to bury. Not the Jews but everyone else. Don't you know your own language?"

So Melanie, too, fell in love with him. Bobby took them to Haifa that afternoon, to a large modern theater with air conditioning that almost worked.

"I know the right seats," said Agram, "where you can feel flashes of air on your neck."

"How about corn?" asked Bobby. "The butter is like water. It all comes in a box that is difficult to crush."

"Why would you want to crush it?"

"It's part of the fun of going to the movies," said Bobby. "Don't you do that over there? My wife did."

They drank the same sweet orange with the popcorn. Bobby fell asleep. He had said in the car going there that loud noises relaxed him. Agram announced the color changes on the screen in a commanding voice. He held onto Melanie's right knee with his left hand, and covered her neck with his arm. Melanie accepted this. What's more, she liked it, though she wasn't able to say why exactly. She felt that his body, while big, lacked any kind of subtlety. No mysterious crevices, no smells that weren't sweat or aftershave, no symbolic anything. That may have been the reason.

67

As far as he was concerned, Agram was unsurprised about Melanie's falling in love with him. He felt it, and gave her his arm. Another reaction would have been more surprising. Had she resisted, perhaps. Still, he might have attributed resistance to a lack of prudence, and deficiency in character. He assumed that women would just succumb. They always had before. His cigar box was all the proof he needed. His *je ne sais quoi* was proven. He looked at her, after the movie ended. Bobby still slept. "Thinking again?"

"Yes," she smiled. "Do you know what I'm thinking?" Her eyes moistened automatically.

"Of course." He smiled a smile of satisfaction. "Don't worry. I will be good to you. And it will help your piece. You can sell it to *Playboy,* not just your small newspaper. Just change the subject a little."

"But what about Cleo?"

"Wait," he said. "We will talk about it later."

He woke Bobby gently. "It is over again," he said. "Melanie and I have some business. You will take us to Samir's."

"Yes sir," said Bobby. "Quite a picture," he said to Melanie. "You Americans know what you're doing. My favorite films," he added.

"What do you think that movie's about?" Melanie asked Agram.

"The world," he said. "Only the world."

Bobby dropped them off at Samir's, a small old hotel between Haifa and Nazareth. The owner smiled at Agram when they entered and said in English, "What is happening?"

"Samir, how is it going?" asked Agram. They slapped hands, they performed a black power handshake. They spoke a few sentences in Arabic. Samir gave them keys. The room they went to was small and simple, but a vase full of bright red roses was on the bedstand. "Have you ever seen these roses in New Jersey?" said Agram. "They are from here." Then he held her very easily, and took over.

He closed the door to the room and pointed for Melanie to go to the bed. "Don't worry," he said. "I will take good care of you. I can make you happy, I know."

She waited anxiously, sitting on top of the light green chenille bedspread, unsure what to expect from him. She had never gone to bed with a man who was so little known to her, and it frightened her to think that she had no idea what would happen. He went to the bathroom and brought out a large white towel, which he opened on top of the bedspread. He took her clothes off carefully, folding them piece by piece, then putting them in a pile on the floor. He unhooked her bra with one hand, then asked if he could look at her. "Stand up and let me see you," he said. "You are very beautiful. Your skins are perfect." He smiled kindly.

She stood up, then sat down again, saying nothing, watching as though it were happening to someone else. Then he took his own clothes off, just as carefully piling them on the floor. He eased her back onto the pillows, kissed her moistly, and said, "In the beginning it is difficult." She looked into his eyes and he smiled at her. The truth was, though, when Agram made love, he was a bull in a china shop. He stumbled, he aimed, he didn't know quite where to go, and it felt as though he were breaking things. He was the kind who can't fit the key into the lock. Despite this, he seemed very proud somehow, and concerned that she be happy. He might have been clumsy, but at least he was gentle and anxious to please. "Was it good for you?" he asked in a few minutes. "Are you OK now?"

"I'm fine," said Melanie shyly. "But what about Cleo? I can't help but worry about her. What will you say?"

"She knows about life," said Agram. "She knows about these things."

"That doesn't matter. Maybe she'll think we betrayed her."

"You are working," he said. "This is research." He laughed, making it seem almost logical. They sat facing each other, naked. Melanie was at the foot of the bed, looking up because the bed sloped downward. Agram faced the window. One eye looked over her shoulder, outside. "I know what I'm doing," he said. "I do not betray anyone. Don't worry."

Melanie felt somewhat relieved. "You must be hungry," he said. "Let's go and eat. They have a very good cook here. Samir's wife. You know, the Palestinians are the best cooks in the Middle East."

"I heard it was the Syrians."

"Not bad," he said. "But we are the real people of the mouth. We are famous."

They dressed quickly, then walked down the stairs. The building seemed shoddier than it had in the room. The room at least held the charm of an old place, where light comes in regularly and softens the angles away. But the darkened stairway, a cold shaft of cement, seemed more like a passageway to a cave than a connection from one inhabited place to another. Melanie shivered. Agram whistled an odd song that sounded both happy and plaintive. He patted her on the shoulder.

"So what do you eat in your America? Tell me. All I know is hot dogs. Though I haven't heard about them in a while."

"The women's movement changed all that."

"Are you making a joke? You American women are a puzzle." He kissed her on her nose.

"It's a big country," she said, as if to explain.

"Not like Nazareth. Here we eat, we drink, we sleep, we marry each other, we watch the world walk by our door. In America, you have no time to think. Everybody's in a rush. For what? Why are you running?"

Melanie reached for his hand. For an instant she wanted the life he described in Nazareth for her own, a simple life where everyone knew what to do and how to do it. If you weren't sure, somebody would tell you. She found his hand. It was dry, strong, something to hold onto.

"What is your wife like?"

"She a very good woman. I told you before."

"What's her name?"

"Why is it so important to know the name?"

They walked into the kitchen and sat down. "Mr. Samir," said Agram. "I would like you to meet an American journalist. From New York, she came to write about us and what we are thinking. Why don't you give her some food to think about."

"Food for thought. An American expression."

"I know," said Agram. "I heard it in the movies."

Cleo was waiting for Melanie, sitting in a coffeehouse a block away from Fuad's. She ran to her as Melanie approached the door. She was nervous, walking back and forth like an anxious horse before a race. "Did you sleep with him?" she shouted.

"Yes," Melanie answered. The question came so rapidly, so unexpectedly, that Melanie hadn't been able to avoid the real answer. She thought she'd have a day to consider what to tell her.

"I was afraid of that. I should have sent Nathan." Cleo paced back and forth in front of Melanie, almost as though she were cutting off Melanie from anything else.

"Wouldn't Agram have had an immediate dislike for Nathan, knowing about your relationship?"

"Nathan doesn't go to bed with men." Cleo was furious. She was not going to accept any explanation. She stood, a bulwark in the desert, making it impossible to walk around her. She spread her legs wide, and her arms extended in straight lines from her body. She looked frightening.

"I'm not Nathan," said Melanie.

"I know. That's why I should have sent him. This could never have happened."

Her logic, though not overwhelming, had to do more with delivery and tone of voice, much like Agram's. Cleo was a seductive woman too. Her persuasion took place because of the size of her character and her overwhelming manner. Like Agram she was somehow bigger than everyone else. Her life seemed crammed full of details that were hard to fathom. These facts lent credence to an otherwise impossible stance or sentence. Cleo's past and her present did not separate in two, like other people's. She was just not like other people. Her four husbands were part of her every word. So was her mysterious, elusive, and yet very concrete other past, a past filled with relatives, facts, even figures that she had no hesitation in spilling forth over the listener. Like Agram, it was impossible to relate to Cleo without loving her.

71

Ten

Letter to William Hall

I know I wrote you only five days ago, but my perceptions here are changing so quickly that I wanted to send you a note while the ideas are fresh, just so you can see the way my thoughts are evolving. You might find my letters hopelessly apolitical—I know that is something you detest, but be patient with me here. I want you to know that Nazareth is a city of a unique and complex kind of romance. The heat, the same heat the engulfed Bogart and Bergman as lovers in Casablanca (not all that far from here) sweeps over everyone who walks through this town. Even in winter, when Nazareth becomes a holy city at Christmas (second to Bethlehem, they say), they tell me it's no different. Lust is everywhere. The camels shake with it, the old men sitting on their stools sway with it still, and the women young and old, rounded from sweet cakes and rich fruit stews, hold the center of this lust. It's a feeling, timeless and ageless, heavy in some places and missing in others, that makes outsiders uncomfortable. It's more a promise than a reality, but the illusion is so great it's impossible not to succumb. The Israelis are different from the Arabs in this way. They seem clean and practical, living on white hills above the twisted old towns. They want the world to be as efficient and well run as an American hospital. They walk through the old sections quickly, stopping infrequently. Religious women from France, nuns mostly, walk briskly too, passing through the streets that are on the way to church, but just passing. Sometimes they seem to feel the strength of temptation and actually run to where they are going.

Scholars, American or English usually, say none of this is so: that the lust is an imagined Western idea, a way of romanticizing Arabs and turning them into compelling animals. And yet it's as real as the penetrating heat of the day, as real as the eyes that follow the stranger around, as real as the hidden messages in all interactions between men and women here. Some say all the Mediterranean is just this way. They dismiss the area with easy answers: it comes from repression, from the Catholic church, from the strict sexual taboos that created an atmosphere of repression. In fact, this is not so. They are not all the same, these men and women living in heat, within reasonable distance from the sea. The Spanish seem to have lost their lust after Don Juan and Goya: Picasso's angles are mathematical in a way that just doesn't exist in Nazareth. In Greece, a place of infinite beauty, there's an aridness that takes over early on, turning the men toward each other for companionship, even dancing. Greece seems to be a country with no women in it. As for the Italians, they are not a subtle society, so their families and their foods and their loves are what they seem to be and no more. Vain men, roosters really, walk in perfectly pressed trousers looking for women to admire them without destroying their creases.

Nazareth is difficult perhaps for someone from a culture of efficiency and scheduling. They don't exist here. A travel agent has an office, but he's usually out to lunch (or even breakfast). Things open and close at will. As for a journalist writing about it all, it's an impossible task. Because this is a city so different from anywhere else I've been that it can't be measured in minutes or hours but in lifetimes. In an unchanging wave of hot days and different people living on top of a hillside, in an endless flow of believers in birthplaces and holiness (and people who seek souvenirs of both), in the core of existence that seems to be at the very heart of the complicated daily lives, contradicting beliefs and values at every turn. In the city's ability to juxtapose ancient truths with modern lies.

I don't mean to alarm you, to leave you with the impression that I am just watching them all fall in love (and falling in love myself). But my daily life is a lot different from the library-intensive existence I'd imagined.

Don't worry: I have an appointment with an Arab intellectual in a few days. Maybe I'll be able to conclude that the Palestinians are thinking about the things you want them to, before long.

Melanie

A few days later Mordecai came to take Melanie to dinner again. Shari revealed that she had known more about Mordecai than she'd let on at first, not because he patrolled the town, but through her friend Miriam, who'd been in love with him while he was still married. One morning when Melanie was dressing, Shari came in, and out of the blue she started talking about how much Miriam had loved Mordecai.

"Miriam is an Israeli cousin of friends of my parents'," said Shari. "When Fuad and I got married and moved to Nazareth, these friends sent us a subscription to the *New Republic* and a good-luck note. In the note they included Miriam's address. I was desperate for friends, so I wrote her a postcard asking if we could meet. Miriam talked and I listened. She was in love with a married man named Mordecai, and she couldn't discuss this with anyone in her own circle because Mordecai's wife was Miriam's best friend Edna's first cousin, and Edna didn't know. By the time their liaison had reached an end, Miriam had given an elaborate blow-by-blow account of her passion for Mordecai. I probably know more about him than his ex."

"Why did they separate? What happened?" asked Melanie.

"Miriam wanted to get married," said Shari. "Mordecai couldn't. Besides, he'd told her that he didn't love her, for reasons she never understood. An El Al pilot asked her to marry him around the same time, and Miriam said yes. They didn't invite us to the wedding."

"Does Mordecai know you? Were you both pretending when he came to pick me up a few days ago?"

"He has no idea I know Miriam," said Shari. "I can't imagine why she would have told him."

Melanie, though she felt she did love Agram, couldn't help waiting for Mordecai with the same set of expectations that accompanied her first date with him. Miriam's love had made him more desirable. Besides, there was something about him that she liked. Not his charm, exactly, but the certainty with which he pursued her.

Melanie did not feel as passive in this as she might: it wasn't as though one or the other would sweep her away forever. Instead, she felt as though she'd been living in a cocoon for years—an untouchable place apart from the world—and this was her chance to experience all that she could. Besides, she could always go back. She thought that foreign men, especially those who didn't quite have full grasp of her language, could be the most perfect of beings, as long as they were able to remain unknown to her. This alone made it seem possible to say that elusive and wonderful thing to each other that couldn't seem to be said in more familiar circumstances. It was easier to talk in foreign places in foreign languages because the words aren't entirely real.

Although she'd already felt some of this with Agram, that did not

75

prevent her from wanting to feel more of the same. Strangers breed optimism, and Melanie felt especially optimistic.

"Miriam said he makes love like a Hasid," said Shari. "Watch out."

"I don't even know what that means. How would you know something like that?"

"By living here. You're exposed to everything. The Hasidim, some of them anyway, have a sheet between them with a small hole three-quarters of the way down. You can imagine," said Shari.

"So why did she love him?"

"Who knows?" said Shari. "I suppose lovemaking isn't everything."

Mordecai did make love like a Hasid. But he took Melanie to another nice dinner first. Schnitzel this time, made from turkey instead of veal. He ordered for both of them, just like before, acting as though he knew her every wish.

The restaurant had music blaring from speakers, loud love ballads that sounded overwhelmingly sad. It seemed to waft over Melanie and Mordecai, out into the Sea of Galilee. "Do you understand the words?" he asked her.

"No," said Melanie. "I can only say a very few things in Hebrew. The basic words like *yes* and *no* and *cat*."

"That won't be of use here," said Mordecai. "How will you understand?"

"It's a problem. Fortunately, many of the people speak English."

"We must learn in school. What's wrong over there? You have no teachers of language?"

"We do, but the languages are generally French or Spanish."

"Don't they know about Hebrew?"

"It's a small country," said Melanie. "Those who want to learn Hebrew do."

"Not all," he said. "You want to learn, don't you?"

After dinner, he took her by the elbow into the back seat of his station wagon and laid her down gently, as though he were resting her on top of a bunch of fragile flowers. They had sex. It was rapid and inoffensive. He was kind, a father helping a child to tie shoes.

76

The sex seemed to make no difference. She was curious about why he bothered, so she asked him during the drive back home.

"What's the matter, you want it again?" he asked. "I am ready."

She figured she'd better wait and see. As it was, the sex made no difference to the way he treated her, or she him. Strangers, they continued with familiar formality, and when he said good night, standing by Fuad and Shari's doorway, he was much like a high school senior bringing his date home intact. He did say, in a soft and confident way, "Don't worry. I'll come again in two nights at eight. Tomorrow I must work. But in two nights we will eat again." Then he winked at her and squeezed her upper arm.

What Melanie didn't understand was why she continued to wait for him. Despite Agram, and her task at hand. She kept reading books about Palestinians, talking to various experts during the day, taping conversations and transcribing them later.

One afternoon, interviewing Palestinians who lived on the West Bank, she ran into Fuad. He sat with a girl under an umbrella that said *Cinzano*. They were sitting, but anyone could feel they were thinking of more. He didn't seem to want to introduce the girl. He looked almost shy, even embarrassed. But Melanie was curious. She walked right up to them and smiled.

"My name is Namati," said the girl. "I am studying philosophy at Beir Zeit college here, and Fuad is helping me to understand."

"Don't exaggerate," said Fuad, feigning modesty. "I'm only listening while you amplify."

"What is *amplify*?"

"Not an easy word. They use it a great deal with rock and roll music. It means to make louder, in that context. Sometimes it means to expound, to elucidate, to clear up, to explain."

"What nice words," she said in clear admiration.

She seemed in love. Fuad sat, the humble and wise master of philosophy and revolution both, his face assuming the expression of modest certainty. He leaned back in his chair, a cafe guru.

"Are you finding out?" he asked Melanie enigmatically.

"I'm trying," she responded in kind.

"All you can do, after all," said Fuad. He explained to Namati,

"We know each other through mutual friends. She interviewed me about Palestinian life, for America."

Namati's amorousness seemed to intensify instantly. "Fuad and I are new acquaintances," she said. "I am only now learning his talents."

"Where did you learn your English?"

"I am a reader of American literature. I have learned much from the living rooms of Henry James," she said.

They appeared to be well suited.

"I am unable to offer you a ride back to Nazareth," said Fuad. "Much as I would like to."

"That's OK. I am meeting someone here, and can take a bus back."

"I believe I know about your appointment from other sources," Fuad said. "Good luck with him."

"How did you hear?"

"Ways," he said. "Would you like to join us now for a midafternoon drink? Some tea? Or are you in a hurry?"

"No. I'm anxious to write up my notes from this morning."

"Good luck," Fuad repeated. "Of course we will see each other again."

"I certainly hope so," said Melanie, willing to play along for intrigue's sake.

"Farewell," said Namati. She waved toward the sky.

Eleven

William Hall, newspaper editor, was a prominent and respected member of the small international community of Catholic Marxist pacifist anarchists, and he thought about peace inordinately. The world community to which he belonged all knew each other. They were on the right side of things in places like Latin America and Africa, and they often won prizes for peace thinking. William Hall's major achievement was an editorial he'd written explaining the Northern Ireland conflict. That editorial had been reprinted in sixteen languages, including Swahili.

A serious man, he was anti-abortion for reasons of faith, but in most other instances his was the voice of perfect reason. He had an overwhelming desire to find out why things happened, and a just as overwhelming fear that this knowledge might destroy every belief that he held. He lived with the fear of fraudulence.

Along with eleven other serious religious leftist intellectuals from America, he'd been on a tour of the Middle East right after the Six Day War. Of the eleven people, there were eight men and three women. According to Hall, the women were more unusual: an ex-nun, a Reconstructionist rabbi, and a radical lesbian theologian of some prominence in divinity school circles. William Hall wrote a long piece that was reprinted in Beirut describing Nazareth as a travesty of a holy city. That piece, with only a line or two of local color, was the reason why Melanie chose to go there. He had said that the nuns walked on tiptoe so as not to disturb the tenuous order of things. Like Melanie, William Hall was a letter writer. He pondered the perfectability of a sentence with the very same seriousness he employed for his war and peace essays. His letters, warm, ironic, and informational, were always neatly typed. He often gave the recipient two word choices, side by side, leaving the final editorial choice. Riddled with ambivalence, William Hall looked nervously on the entire prospect of decision making. His martini held both a twist of lemon and an olive. So deciding between Israelis and Palestinians had been an impossible matter. William Hall, editor of the *American Journal*, wrote to Melanie:

It was good to hear from you, although your letter was confusing. I am sending you this one express (is there express mail there? I could not secure a definite answer on this) in the hopes of reaching you with some very general responses and advice (suggestions). It sounds as though you are being affected (moved) somehow by what you are seeing, though I am incapable of understanding *just how*. Have you formed an opinion (perspective) of the situation, or are you leaving judgment (analysis) for your homecoming? Have you read any contemporary intellectuals from the area that might be worth our pursuing to write for the *Journal*?

One problem I have always had with this situation (conflict)—and I throw it out not to confuse you, but rather to add more information to your store—is that both are underdogs (disadvantaged). You know that we religious intellectuals (leftists in particular, I suppose) have a tendency to believe that underdogs have more to do with holiness (truth). After all, Jesus was pretty down and out in the end, no matter what happened later. Perhaps this is a difficult concept for you as a Jew to recognize, though surely underdogs play a significant role in some strain of Judaism as well. (If I am misinformed on this, forgive me.)

Israelis, for all of their aggression and hostility (problematic natures), became the way they did for reasons of international callousness, and worse. We are all to blame for World War II, God knows. Catholics are especially vulnerable (culpable). Official Catholicism didn't know what to do with the Jews for centuries, how to understand them. Besides, everyone needs a state. (Or do they? What of the Armenians, for instance? But then, they have the Soviet Union.) It is human nature, instinct, the way of the world.

Palestinians, too, are underdogs. With years of living in camps behind them, with no clear pathway for the future, with all of the problems of trying to devise a solution to the impossible difficulty of displacement (land loss), they, too, have a cause worthy of support.

80

I would like to suggest—this is only a suggestion, but a good (helpful) one—that you visit Mr. Fouzi el-Ahmad, in the West Bank. He addressed the eleven of us after the Six Day War in such a moving and effective way that we all wrote about it on our return. He is the kind of speaker who makes sense.

Some personal thoughts about the West Bank: This place, these last ten years, has achieved nothing short of mythic status. Many Orthodox Jews have adopted it as their personal cause (vendetta), claiming that God wanted them to be there. Fervent individuals of one sort or another have gone to live for what they hope is forever, shouting the words *Judaea* and *Sumarea* as if they were newly discovered battle cries. Still others, Palestinians who have lived on that land for generations, are just average people with clean kitchen floors and children in grammar school (some sort of educational facilities). It's easy to forget about average people. Bayonets and bombings seem to be all there is on the West Bank. In fact, it's a civilized and beautiful area, overlooking the ancient hills of Judaea. The people there are confused. They were once an almost logical part of the world around them. Not happy, perhaps, but where in the world is there a neighborhood of happy people? (Lichtenstein?) Now they are neither here nor there. Not Jordanian, not Israeli, even though the last war says otherwise, they are also forbidden to fend for themselves. They are the enemy, and this happened too quickly. A charming people with a long history of intelligence, poetry, and excellent food, they have become angry (frustrated? oppressed?) of late. They nod at each other with an awareness that only comes from common battles.

There's a lot of money in the West Bank too. It behooves the concerned consciousness to paint a picture of dusty poverty like in Egypt or Syria (even Yemen). But the West Bank isn't that sort of place. It can be dusty, but it isn't poor. The children are not ragged (diseased) and pathetic: they look bright and well cared for. It's a suburb of Jerusalem, really, with many doctors, lawyers, teachers, and small-business owners. The houses are beautiful. Old Arab designs, with open courtyards and lemon (perhaps quince) trees, the kind with interior patios, hand-painted tiles of flying birds (eagles), and family samovars of pounded brass. In one house, bigger than his neighbors', is Mr. Fouzi el-Ahmad. Do go see him. It will be worth it.

Melanie had prepared carefully to meet with el-Ahmad, asking around about his interests and beliefs, and reading several interviews that had been done by Jean-Paul Sartre. She knocked on his heavy, carved door, and heard the word "Enter." It was said with the tone of God speaking at heaven's gates.

"Enter," he repeated, even louder the second time. Melanie was

81

taken off guard. She had expected humility, a quality William Hall admired. She pushed the door open as fast as she could but it was heavy.

She walked inside and immediately felt the dark and dampness of the hall. It took her a few minutes to adjust to the light and the unexpected length of the entranceway. But she could see, at the end, a large, bright room where el-Ahmad sat, right in front of the window. She could smell the flowers and the incense as she walked toward him.

He sat, small and dark, the kind of man who believes that large chairs add to his stature. The chair back was so high, it made him look like Humpty Dumpty. He seemed unnaturally short, plump legs dangling over the edge of the chair, like an elf on top of a mushroom.

Melanie leaned forward to shake his hand. He looked surprised, broadly pursed his lips as if to kiss her hand, decided not to and thrust his hand out instead, upward in an Indian gesture of peace. He did not rise from his throne, managing to peer down at her even though she towered over his chair. The peering was directed toward her feet.

"I am so terribly pleased to be afforded the privilege of meeting with you," he said. His voice held the official condescension of a British diplomat. "May I offer you some of our finest Arabic coffee? Do you know that we make it with cardamom seeds? A wonderful thing, that. Your superior, Mr. William Hall, is a man I respect very greatly. His epistle on your assignment arrived some days ago. Those Catholics are an admirable breed. I am a Christian myself. And you? Polish perhaps?"

He called for his housekeeper by leaning forward in his chair so that his right foot touched the floor. Then he stepped hard on a buzzer under the rug. The maid came quickly, a pretty woman. "The young lady has agreed to sample our Arabic coffee," he said. "And I will have my usual Earl Grey. Please don't quarter the lemon. I want circles, not wedges. The wedges are far too wasteful. She's a frivolous girl," he said to Melanie. Then he waved her away by moving his right hand in the air rapidly, as if he were shooing flies. She ran quickly. He turned toward Melanie again. "Now how can I be of service to a young lady so charming as yourself?"

El-Ahmad looked impressive. His fingernails were pink and white, manicured with clear, flawless polish. His hair was dark and shining with oils; his skin exuded a tautness achieved from regular use of French soaps and expensive conditioners. "How many I help you?" he repeated. "I would be glad to inform you of the history of my people. We are an old and proud society with a rich tradition. Even our humblest of citizens have a poetic facility."

She reached into her briefcase for her list of questions. "Don't bother with those," he said. "I will tell you what you need. You don't even have to ask. I am familiar with the needs of foreign journalists. The answers are all on the tip of the tongue." He extended his tongue forward, very neatly out of his mouth, then replaced it with a closemouthed laugh.

"Can you talk a little about solutions?"

"I assume you are referring to the Israeli problem."

"And the Palestinian one."

"We Palestinians have no problem," he said with confidence. "We are in the process of evolving our own plans for statehood. I'm afraid the term *problem* will then apply elsewhere. For our state will be of a somewhat different nature than what our neighbors may have in mind." He launched into a lengthy explanation of the differences between monarchies, democracies, socialism, and communism, explaining the pros and cons of all four. He concluded by saying, "Of course, Mr. Arafat has no desire to be a monarch or even the sort of autocratic governor symptomatic of a modern democracy. He is just not that kind of fellow."

"How do you see your role in all of this?" she asked him.

"I assume I will function in some sort of advisory capacity. It will be my pleasure to serve my people."

"What would be your area?"

"It doesn't matter all that much, as mine is a multifaceted expertise."

"What have you done until now?"

"I came very close to winning several prizes for peace. But then I suppose you have made yourself familiar with my numerous accomplishments."

"Do you have a family? The house seems very quiet."

"Of course, my dear. This is a land where the nuclear family is flourishing, even among our enemies. They are all on vacation out of the country. We do travel, you know. They are at a well-known coastal resort. For security reasons, I'd rather not say where they are."

"Who might those enemies be?"

"You know them as well as I," he said.

"Has the Israeli government been good to you?" Melanie raised her eyebrows, and her voice.

"I have many friends who are Israelis. We grew up together. Some of my family lives in Haifa. They've been in business there for generations. Israelis are my brothers."

"What do you think of the state of Israel?"

"I have no intentions whatsoever of pushing these people into the sea, if that's what you're wondering about." He laughed. "In case you are familiar with that phrase, let me inform you that it is simply government propaganda. No one desires it here. Mr. Qaddafi, now there's a man who is somewhat extreme; he may have strong intentions, but even he has not mentioned the sea in some years now. As I'm sure you know, his Libya and our Mediterranean are quite far apart. The rest of us are more reasonable people. We are not warlike. The Palestinians are far from being Turks. We are as calm as is possible for a people dispossessed. All that we want is a home."

"What kind of home?"

"That remains to be mutually determined. We are a people's people," he explained. "We want what is good for the majority. It remains for our majority to make that decision. And we will."

"What do you think of Mr. Arafat?"

"A courageous man, as well as a fine leader. He will be the very first ruler of Palestine."

"What is he like as a person?"

"The same as you and me," he said with the kind of smile that often accompanies incomplete remarks. "The only difference is that he's somewhat more successful."

84

As he spoke, the doorbell rang, playing the opening notes of "Rockabye Baby." "Brahms," said el-Ahmad.

"I hadn't noticed a doorbell," said Melanie.

"It is only for guests who know me well. It is hidden beneath the welcome mat. I have always believed that the foot is an underutilized appendage. We place too much emphasis on hand techniques." He then shouted into the air, "Go." Footsteps sounded quickly to the door. *"Bonjour bonjour bonjour!"* yelled an exuberant voice, deep and promising.

"He will be my second interview of the day," said Mr. el-Ahmad. "And tonight come the Germans. The gentleman who is engaged in arriving is the finest reporter on the Middle East in the entire world. He is, of course, French. The French, as you are no doubt aware, are well known for their general quality of thought. Not that the English are far behind." He sighed. "You Americans are not an intellectual people, but you are still young. You are efficient, however," he said. "And you do have a certain indiscriminate enthusiasm."

The reporter entered the room on the heels of the maid, glancing over her as if she were just one of an infinite line of conquests. She returned his glance on her way out, as adoring as he might wish. He was a tall man, head held higher than necessary as if to communicate well-bred vanity. He wore a perfect suit: hand-sewn buttonholes, exquisite material the color of the desert at dusk. He looked as though he were just dressed for this moment. He had a gray and black goatee, well trimmed, and a general air of elegance.

"Habibi," he said to Mr. el-Ahmad, who turned to Melanie and stage-whispered, "That means friend."

El-Ahmad looked very pleased, as though finally a guest had entered that was worthy of his time. He sat straighter in his chair and spread his arms wide. The reporter then walked across the room into the outstretched arms. El-Ahmad jumped up. Standing, he seemed even closer to the ground. The reporter engulfed him with an easy and graceful swooping.

Gently, el-Ahmad was dropped to his seat, and gently, too, the reporter slid into his own chair, legs crossed so that the creases of his pants hung in perfect straight lines from the knees. El-Ahmad remembered his role as host. "Monsieur Frederick Fedaille," he said, "permit me to introduce you to an American reporter from the city of New York."

"How do you do," said Melanie, extending her hand once again.

"*Enchanté,*" said Fedaille. He kissed her hand dryly. "You must be new. Are you the new stringer for the *New York Times*, perchance?" He looked doubtful that this could be possible. "Perhaps a wire service."

"No," she answered, embarrassed. "It's a small paper, leftist in orientation." She mumbled the word *leftist,* uncertain of Mr. Fedaille's politics.

"Aha," he answered vaguely, then turned away. His momentary interest vanished, and he made no pretense of caring about her. He turned toward el-Ahmad and began a very rapid conversation in French. They both seemed to speak in long sentences, punctuated with frequent affirmative head-shaking, as well as mutual pats on the back. El-Ahmad interrupted only once, to call out "Whiskey," and then continued. When the whiskey came, the host became gracious again.

"May I offer you some of your very own Jack Daniels?" he said. "We would be most pleased if it were possible for you to join us."

"Yes, do," added Monsieur Fedaille. This was said in the manner of a brief but pointed farewell address. Melanie understood that she was to leave immediately. She stood.

"But where are you staying?" asked Monsieur Fedaille.

"Nazareth."

"You know it is quite an important city for Christians." His English was impeccable.

"I have heard that."

"And what about Nablus," added Mr. el-Ahmad. "The presence of a French man and an American lady here in our small village indicates something of this very village's importance as well, does it not? Surely you would agree to this."

"*C'est vrai,*" said Fedaille. "True, true," he added in English.

"Gentlemen," said Melanie, turning to leave.

"You are leaving," said el-Ahmad. *"Quel dommage.* I'm so sorry."

"Thank you for your time," she answered.

"If you wouldn't mind, I would appreciate receiving tear sheets of those sections where I am quoted," he asked. "You may care to send me the entire article, if you like."

"Of course."

"I hope I was of some small service," he said. "If I can be of further assistance, do not hesitate. I will give you my private telephone. It's a number I entrust to a very few. Call me for whatever reasons, no matter how personal." He smiled at Fedaille when he said this, then turned back to Melanie. "I await your word."

"Au revoir, ma petite journaliste," said Fedaille, waving his hand vigorously, *"et bonne chance."*

"Good-bye," she said. "Good-bye."

Twelve

The next afternoon, Melanie invited Shari to accompany her to Haifa, where she had made an appointment to interview a prominent professor of nuclear physics, an Israeli who'd been living there for generations. He claimed to know the answers for peace. Now an elderly man, he took out ads in international newspapers on occasions of peril and indicated in a language that was both scientific and humane that the solution to peace was biochemical. Some famous intellectuals, American leftists in particular, felt that he might have something there. William Hall was one of his admirers. Hall had personally arranged the meeting before Melanie left for Israel, having once met the scientist at a convocation on Molecules, Mozart, and Armed Struggles in Salzburg.

The women arranged to meet after Melanie's interview, which turned out to be short and not altogether helpful. It took place in the professor's office at Israel's MIT, the Technion. Professor Aviv had a chair there. His office was cluttered with old copies of *New Scientist*, a popular English science weekly, *Scientific American*, and the *Western Reserve Alumni News*. The professor seemed tired and distracted. He was wearing a tie that was spotted with egg stains.

"Have I already sent you all of my articles?" he asked her. "If not, I will put you on my international mailing list. Two hundred and ninety-four people," he said. "Including four Japanese intellectuals. I met them in Haifa. I was a professor for one year in America, at Western Reserve in Ohio. Not bad there. Too cold. I was glad to

89

get home. Can you imagine?" He thrust an old manila folder covered with ink and fingerprints into her hands. It was filled with poorly Xeroxed articles. "If you wouldn't mind returning it to me when you're done," he asked. "I need it for the other journalists. There are many of you. It is self-explanatory," he continued. "I've said it all in that file. Call me if you have questions. I have no time now to answer." He smiled, then stood up for her to leave at once. "All the best and good luck," he said.

She was disappointed in the meeting's brevity, and walked slowly to the cafe to meet Shari, who was already waiting there. Shari looked younger than her thirty-one years. She seemed rested, almost comfortable sitting in the cafe chair. She didn't usually look so at ease.

"I'm in love," she said with great emotion. "I'm in love," she repeated in case Melanie had missed it the first time.

"We all are," answered Melanie. "It seems to be a way of life around here."

"It's not what you think, not the same as your transitory comings and goings. I live here, no matter what I might think about that. This is my home, complete with a husband and his mother. They count on me, though for what I'm not quite sure. But I am tied to them inextricably. Fuad and I drift apart and together as if our destinies are one and the same. Neither of us can afford to relinquish our hold. This is not a physical question—it's far more serious. We have created our own elaborate system for belonging, a system that could destroy our very selves if something happened to it. And now I'm afraid I am ready to do just that. I'm not so worried about what will happen to Fuad: it's the part of myself that will vanish with him that I fear losing. I am Fuad in a way after all these years. And he, I suppose, is part of me too."

"How are you planning this act of destruction?"

"By telling him that I'm in love."

"Haven't you been in love before?"

"Yes. But it never meant much. Besides, I do love Fuad too. But this is different."

"What makes you say that?" Melanie leaned forward over the table, wondering what Shari could possibly be building toward.

"It's always been with men before. And even an Israeli man would not be as upsetting to Fuad as my loving another woman."

"You're in love with a woman?" Melanie sounded as if she found this hard to believe.

"So is Fuad."

"You know?"

"Not really, but I suspected as much. He often has his liaisons. I don't think it's very important though unless you both love the same woman."

Shari launched into her theory on this. "You know though that for those of us who are American feminists, not quite freed from the taboos of our age, having sex with a sister is more often understood as a political statement rather than an act of pure desire. For a woman to say she's in love with another woman in Nazareth is to say something so explosive as to be nearly unfathomable. In Nazareth, it seems to me that sex is seen as a male idea, with some reference made to the women involved, that reference being merely a form of politeness. Besides," said Shari, ending her speech, "she is beautiful. Intelligent and taut. An unusual person, with strength and energy. She feels nothing but hope for our situation, and hope is what I think I'm missing with Fuad."

"Tell me more about her," Melanie said, curious.

"I'd rather you met her yourself," said Shari. "I have invited her to join us here. I called her when you were with the professor and said we would be sitting at this cafe. She'll come by any minute. I really want you to meet her. It seems like an important part of the picture. You'll be surprised. Have you yourself ever loved a woman?"

"Of course I have," said Melanie. "We have all been in love with other women, haven't we?"

"Not everyone is so conscious of that," said Shari. "Who was she?"

"She was thirteen, and so was I. An Italian. She was the most beautiful person I'd ever seen, with green eyes and a telephone voice. We could talk to each other for hours. I was anxious to be a woman then, and she already was. Her breasts were white and full and perfect, and mine were still nonexistent. I'm sure I loved her because she was so much more mature than I.''

"Did she love you too?"

"I was never quite sure. She said she did, but she said a lot of things, and it was difficult for me to gauge her honesty. She was a storyteller.''

"How long did it last?"

"It never quite finished, though I haven't seen her in years.''

"Do you know where she is?"

"I've always known. She lives in Hawaii now, unhappily married to someone who went to grammar school with us. She married him out of retaliation. Her high school boyfriend married someone else. She called me once five years ago and said she was in New York. She suggested we meet, then never showed up. We were always afraid of our love.''

"Do you miss her?"

"I miss everyone I've ever loved.'' As she said that, Melanie wondered whether someday she would miss Agram or Mordecai or even both of them. Suddenly, Yael appeared. She slid into her chair with an unusual gracefulness.

At first, Yael gave the impression of someone slight. Looking at her more carefully, though, revealed a piercing thinness; she seemed to have the kind of intensity that had no edges but just bore through whatever she chose to look at. She seemed to have the same kind of self-confidence as Fuad. Shari introduced them.

"Yael is a kibbutznik,'' she said. "She works in the kibbutz sandal shop, and we met when I bought a pair. We've been meeting for a while now.''

"For how long?"

"Eleven months. Nearly a year,'' said Shari. "We met last spring.''

"Have you ever been out of the country, Yael?"

"To Boston, where my mother was born. She still has family there, though she herself emigrated over thirty years ago. She still

92

lives on the kibbutz she helped found," said Yael. "A different husband, but the kibbutz is the same."

"What happened to her husband?"

"She left him for an authentic Sabra," said Yael. "She became very much a purist here."

"Do you both live in the same place?"

"Not at all. My kibbutz is too industrialized for my mother. We use outside Arab labor. She's a real pioneer, a strong woman who went to college in Illinois. Israelis have a lot in common with American midwesterners. They are puritanical stoics, so she feels right at home here."

Shari gave Yael an admiring look, pleased with her summation. Melanie was intrigued.

"How do you feel about kibbutz life? Can you see yourself living somewhere else?"

"I'm not so different from my mother," said Yael. "I am a purist too, and kibbutz comes closest to my own sense of ideals."

"But what about the Arabs here? What do they think about kibbutz, and what does the kibbutz think of them?"

"Some say kibbutz is a place of false justice, a kind of restricted egalitarianism. For me, though, its success is linked to the homogeneity of its population. That way, the principles can be put into effect without much difficulty."

"What are the principles?"

"They are largely Marxist in nature."

"Do you have to be a Jew to be Marxist?"

"Of course not. But to live as a kibbutznik in this particular part of the world, it is not just expected, it is also necessary. Anything else would cause conflict. Besides, Arabs who want to live on kibbutz can always go to Japan." She looked satisfied with her solution.

"Why Japan?"

"The Japanese came to study us twenty years ago, and now they have kibbutzim of their own, near Kyoto. They are clever, industrious people. I'm sure the Arabs would be happier there than here. Not nearly the problems."

"Wouldn't Japan be more alien than here?"

93

"How can they know until they try? My mother took to this country like a duck out of water."

"But you said that she studied in the Midwest, that the Midwest and Israel are similar."

"The Arabs call themselves Orientals," said Yael. "Maybe you didn't know that. Besides, I thought journalists were just supposed to record. Isn't having an advocacy position, even arguing, contrary to your job? Do you want to know what I think, or don't you?"

"I'm not sure," Melanie replied. "I feel as though my knowing wouldn't help much of anything."

"With what?"

"With applying the knowledge somehow."

"It's all simple," said Yael. She looked very efficient, like a schoolteacher telling a class the right answer. "You just have to write your story. Your responsibility ends there."

"What makes you so sure?"

"I don't agree," said Shari. "I believe in activism. It's the basis for change."

"But what is she going to change?" said Yael. "She lives there. You can't change anything from there. The most you can do is write an article. Who's going to read it anyway?"

"How do you think the Arabs here view their options?" said Melanie, refusing to become entirely discouraged.

"They won't be pragmatic and leave," said Yael in a voice that lacked even the slightest flicker of doubt. "They discuss what should have happened in 1948, not what is happening today. I think they ought to recognize their reality, create a viable alternative given the limitations that exist in terms of Israel, and then negotiate. Come up with a solution. That's what the Jews did. I am," she said in an uncompromising way, "not at all afraid to negotiate. Fair is fair."

"Can we change the subject?" asked Shari. "Let's talk about sandals or weather, or even Israeli feminism."

"I'm sorry, Shari," said Yael. "Discussing the Arabs seems to bring out the worst in me, though I don't know why it should. I suppose I feel guilty, and resentful." She seemed to soften as she spoke, to become more real. Her eyes were beautiful, clear, and

94

green, and her body charged with energy. "Tell me what your experience has been here, Melanie. Have you found out what you wanted to know?" She looked Melanie right in the eyes, in a way that was disarming.

Melanie looked back at her just as directly. "Personally, it's been interesting," she said. "Professionally, though, I'm still not sure."

"What happened personally?"

"It's the first time that I've been really exposed to lives so different from my own," she said. "It's been a disconcerting experience."

"Can you see yourself ever living here?"

"I'm not sure I'd belong."

"No one does. That's one of the charms of Israel," she said. "You might be very happy here. Feel free to come to kibbutz to visit. It's another kind of life here."

They continued their conversation for some time, sitting on top of the city, with a view overlooking the sea. The sun was still high in the sky when they sat down to talk, but by the time they got up to leave, it had already set behind the hills, and the Haifa lights, scattered up and down the hill, were nearly all on by the time they said good night.

Thirteen

Nathan walked in the door of Melanie's room and took over. It was nine at night when he arrived unannounced, and Melanie was writing up her interview notes from that afternoon. Fuad led him to the room in silence. "Your dresser really is in the wrong place," he began. "And good evening." Then he continued, "If you moved it all the way over, against the wall on your left, you'd have much more room for standing."

His manner was both brisk and efficient. He wore tight black pants, making it necessary for him to pull them up from the knees before he sat down on the end of Melanie's bed, where she was stretched out working. When Cleo had originally described Nathan to Melanie, she had likened him to Richard Burton, part of the school of pockmarked men who use their skin as an indicator of sexual prowess. Ravaged themselves, it was a sure sign that they had the potential to ravage others. Cleo never mentioned Nathan's voice, however.

It had little to do with listening. He spoke with the tenor of a ringing smoke detector. He wore a thick gold identification bracelet on his right hand with *Nathan* written across it in curlicued script. When he saw Melanie looking at it, he said, "Twenty-four karat. They don't have this available in your country. I have twelve thousand dollars U.S. worth of jewelry. Many necklaces and two family rings. And what about your dresser?" he concluded, as if owning the jewelry gave him added authority.

97

"This is not really my room," she told him. "Shari and Fuad have been kind enough to let me stay, but I'm just a guest, grateful to have a room so close to the center of town."

"They'll appreciate your giving them some good advice," said Nathan. "Not everyone is aware of how to place furniture. In India I happened to have worked in a furniture store for a brief period. The store, of course, belonged to a relative, my uncle. I often designed the windows, which faced an affluent and well-trafficked street. This was in Bombay, a very big city, so many people saw my windows. How I put the tables and chairs was copied all over India. I was the one who made the decision about the direction for the couch, whether to put the coffee table on the left or the right, where to position the lamp. I know the answers to these questions well. You don't even have to tell your hosts that I made this suggestion. You can take all the credit for this improvement. Tell them you worked in a furniture store once. They will be unable to verify that."

"I'd rather ask them if they want to move things before I make any suggestions."

"Too cautious," said Nathan, disapproving. He clucked. "Nothing will get done. You would have made much more room for standing," he repeated.

"What are you doing here?" Melanie asked him.

"To express Cleo's profound and insufferable misery with you, because of the recent turn of events. You know, I am sure, about what I am referring. I am her emissary, her bearer of unhappy tidings."

"You are not being clear."

"I am referring, of course, to your needless and immoral encounter with Agram. He is a married man. No good can come from this." With these last two words, Nathan's voice escalated even higher, for emphasis. He was nearly shrieking. "Unnecessary hurts are being inflicted by you, out of cruel and unthinking callousness. Your own momentary needs had a devastating effect on someone else's life. Why are you inflicting so much pain?"

"Isn't this role a conflict of interest for you?" asked Melanie. "Wouldn't it make much more sense for you to use this opportunity to strengthen your own position with Cleo, rather than aid someone else's cause?''

"I am in love with her," he said, still shrieking. "I just want her happiness. If she wants Agram, then she should have him. I don't want you to stand in her way. My own feelings are secondary in this matter. She is the superior being.''

"What about my needs?''

"Less important," declared Nathan. "You are just not as significant an individual. She deserves more at this stage of her life. She has suffered through many marriages. Her children gave her pain. She is entitled to happiness.'' He said this in a manner that was somehow not offensive, as if he were delivering a litany of adoration, rather than just talking.

"And what do you want in all of this?''

"I am hopelessly in love with her. Of course, she is also in love with me.''

"Then I must ask again, why are you so interested in the Agram situation?''

"I am speaking now on her behalf. We are one voice," said Nathan.

"You really don't see him as your competition?''

"Not at all," he answered. "Agram is an older gentleman, and I am but thirty-seven. He has a wife and large children. I can afford generosity. He and Cleo are only passing fancies. Nothing serious. She told me so. Besides," he said with a confident air, "Cleo likes sex, and Agram, as you must know, has some very grave problems in that area. Let them have fun. I am a good sport, as well as a superior lover. Even the Jews in India are masters of the *Kama Sutra*. Are you acquainted with those techniques?''

"I've heard of them, though have never experienced them firsthand," answered Melanie. "I'm more interested in the problems of Agram. What are they?''

"You will find the answer soon enough," he said. "It may not be immediately apparent, but if you continue to pursue the relationship, the problem will surface. And for you it will be most humiliating.''

"Do you know this from firsthand experience?''

"A most outrageous idea," said Nathan. "Whyever would I have sex with a man anyway? All of the women in the world are mine. Are you implying that there is something peculiar about my character? What makes you raise this? Did Agram say something? Don't you find me attractive?" He stared into her eyes.

"I just don't understand why I didn't notice the sexual idiosyncrasies or inadequacies of Agram myself. How did they escape me? And just why are you so sure of them? Maybe Cleo told you that to make you feel less threatened."

"You were swept up in a wave of blinding passions." Nathan seemed more doubtful than before. "Let's return to your homosexual remark. Were you maligning me in some way? Would you like to see for yourself? You will not be sorry. As you might imagine, I am a master."

"I have not doubted your success with women, though I don't feel the urge to succumb," said Melanie. "Besides, that would make things really impossible. Your relationship with Cleo would be totally destroyed."

"She doesn't have to know," said Nathan. "Some things I keep from her."

"I thought you were in love with her. Wouldn't having sex with me be a betrayal?"

"I would be proving a point," said Nathan. "That's different."

"Speaking of points, I wonder if you have an opinion about how the Arabs here see their future." Melanie felt nervous and uncertain.

"Cleo told me that was the topic of your report, and you yourself made reference to the subject to me not long ago," he began. He did have an opinion, long-winded and high-pitched. "The Arabs think," he began. He seemed to go on and on, presenting the Indian-Jewish perspective. "We are all members of the Third World," he concluded. "It is our responsibility to band together and make a revolution."

"So you are a revolutionary."

"Not at all," he said. "But I am sympathetic to the responsibilities I have as a citizen of this part of the world. The Near East and Far East all meet in the Middle."

"I thought the Near East and Middle East were the same."

"You know little," said Nathan. "As I suspected."

"I am trying to learn. Do you feel more affinity with the Arabs or the Israelis?"

"Hard to say," said Nathan. "Of course you must have heard of Gandhi. He would have like them both. I am in a unique position of being both Jew and Indian. That is part of my attractiveness."

Nathan drew an iridescent red comb from his back pocket. He combed his wet and shining hair very slowly, concentrating on it with great intensity, breathing loudly. He faced the mirror. "If you would move this where it belonged," he said, "the reflection would be more accurate. Then you could really see how you looked."

He smiled at Melanie, kissed her wetly on her cheek, and left.

Fourteen

Agram eats as though he were solving the cure for cancer with each bite. Like bridge or golf for some, it is a crucial central focus for his life: the difference, though, is he makes his eating seem important to others around him. He couldn't meet without eating. In order to talk, he had to be in a restaurant. He responded to Melanie's early-morning request for a meeting by agreeing to pick her up at night, to go to eat.

For once, he drove himself. The car was different than the one Bobby drove, a big pink and gray Cadillac. Melanie looked more softly defined. Her hair had grown in the weeks since she'd come to Nazareth, and she wore it up but loosely, so tendrils of curls fell softly down her neck. Her earrings, silver bells from the Arab market, swayed across her neck and jangled. Her eye makeup was black lines of kohl drawn inside the eyelids, Eastern style, and the perfume had quickly become part of her being. Even her smile seemed less simple. She wore a dress instead of a skirt and blouse, something loose and transparent, from Greece. Blue and white embroidery covered the yoke, and it hung gracefully, giving her figure some length.

Agram, too, looked as though he'd paid more attention than usual. He wore shoes instead of sandals, and his pants were dark rather than the light ones he wore every day. His shirt, loose and clean, was a very light blue. He didn't look handsome quite, but he looked strong and serious, a little like a Roman hero. He held the wheel loosely, and asked Melanie to tell him about her ex-husband while he drove. "It's not that I didn't love him," she said. "But we couldn't get along. That was a surprise to both of us. We argued about everything: what we should do on our vacation, which movie to see, what kind of couch to buy for the living room. The arguing escalated in a very short time, and finally neither of us could stand it."

"Why not let him win?" said Agram. "Maybe you could still be married. Why fight?"

"Control," explained Melanie. "Both our therapists said it was about control. Knowing didn't help, though. Neither of us was willing to compromise."

"What is control?" asked Agram. "Tell me. I want it." He laughed knowingly, and so did she. She felt more relaxed than ever before, though she wasn't sure why.

For once, she did most of the talking as they drove through the very dark night. It was just eight o'clock, but only an occasional car provided some sense that they were not completely alone. At last, they came to the restaurant. As she expected, the owner greeted Agram with the usual enthusiasm. He, too, was an oversized man, only his shirt was so tight on his body it seemed drawn. "Who is this?" he said in English, filling the words with innuendo. He pronounced *this* as though it were a very important question. Then he raised his eyebrows, pointed to Melanie, and circled his lips with his tongue.

"A journalist," answered Agram, smiling. Agram knew that *journalist* could mean many things.

"Aha aha aha," exclaimed the restaurant owner. He did too. "America. How do you like our Nazareth?"

"We aren't there, are we?"

"Smart girl," said the restaurant owner. "We are someplace else," he exclaimed happily. "But Nazareth is my real home."

"Where are we anyway?" she asked.

"A place," said the owner. "If not a place, then what?"

"He went to the American college in Beirut," said Agram. "You think we are peasants. We are not. How many have you met here who have studied?"

104

"Have you?"

"Only life," he said.

"Agram is an expert," said the owner. "A doctor of life."

"Bring food," commanded Agram kindly. He spread his right arm in a semicircle around the room, indicating the expanse of culinary possibilities.

"You can trust me," said the owner. "It will be perfect."

"What is his name?"

"I didn't tell you before?"

"You forgot."

"Of course not. I have not forgotten his name at all. You have."

"You never told me."

"How could I not tell you? It's important."

"What is it?"

"Sam to you."

"What to other people?"

"Why is it so important that you know everything all the time? I have learned many things from the Jews," said Agram. "A Jew never answers, he asks."

"Someone else has to answer."

"Do they?" he said. "Do they?"

This restaurant had much in common with the place Melanie had eaten her first night out in Nazareth. It was a wide, empty room with Formica picnic tables placed at random, photographs and paintings of deer in the woods, ships at sea, a lighthouse, steering wheels, driftwood, and John F. Kennedy. A wall rug showed four smiling dogs playing poker. The colors in the room were light green and gray, and there were no windows. The restaurant did have outside seating cafe-style, but it was dark and there were no candles on the tables to make this possible at night. Some of the chairs had been placed upside down on the tables, but not all, as if this, too, had been done randomly. A red and white sign, *Coca-Cola*, hung over the entranceway in welcome.

"Why are you always thinking?" Agram said this more gently than usual, as if he had a reason. He reached out and touched Melanie's arm. "What good does it do? Too much thinking is no help. And it just makes the others uncomfortable." He kept holding her arm between wrist and elbow, in a grasp that was a cross between an embrace and an arm hold.

"Don't you ever think?" Melanie didn't move her arm, though she wasn't sure what he was doing.

"What kind of question? Of course I am thinking."

"About what?"

"Would I tell the answer?"

"Why not?"

"You are impossible. Maybe someone can give you money to ask questions. They might pay you."

"I've got that kind of job."

"So what that you're thinking? You're still sitting in the chair, hungry. It doesn't help. You can think and think and think, and nothing changes."

"Then how do you change things?"

"That's another problem."

"And what is your answer?"

"All you want are answers." His eye seemed to wander around the room as though he were checking on the possibility of other listeners. There were three old men playing a board game in an opposite corner, but they seemed oblivious.

"Just tell me how to change things."

"I'll tell you something important. Change has nothing to do with thinking. Do you think Mr. Kissinger spent his time thinking? Or President John F. Kennedy? Or Bobby? Those are people who managed to do more than you and me. And they didn't waste their time sitting and thinking. When they wanted thinking, they just paid somebody else."

"Is that what you do?"

"I'm doing my own," said Agram.

"I believe it."

"What do you mean by that?"

Sam and his helper, a thin man dressed just like Sam in black pants and white shirt, placed dishes on the table with great seriousness. Oil, shining and majestic, slid over the food in a way that lent it harmony. All the food dripped with additional juiciness. Little dishes and big ones covered the table as both Sam and his helper described each dish.

"It is called *mezze*, my little girl," said Sam. "That's Arabic for appetizer. And here is the *pièce de résistance*. This is my mother's most famous dish, learned by every woman in my family, taught to perfection by the mistress of this dish herself. This is our . . ." Here he paused for enough seconds to make Melanie wonder what he could possibly be handing her. "I do not know the word in English. In fact, I would be surprised if there were any English equivalent at all to this miraculous dish, in word or deed. We call it *kibbee bi libbaneh*. I'll write it down for you." He took his ballpoint out of his pocket and wrote down the words on a paper-thin napkin.

"There is not an English translation," said Agram definitively.

"There could not be," said Sam.

"What's in it, then?" she asked them.

"You must wait," said Sam. "This cannot be eaten at first. You must build the palate. It comes after the olives, the turnips pickled in beet juice, the other things."

"It looks unusual," said Melanie, gazing at what appeared to be boiled mouse meat drenched in a loose white substance. She wondered about actually eating it.

"Beautiful is the right word," said Agram. "Your people have no culture. You don't know food."

"Beautiful," echoed Sam. "More beautiful than your Mona Lisa, or Rembrandt."

"And wait until the taste," said Agram. "This is something you don't forget."

"I look forward to it," she said, apprehensive.

"This is a once-in-a-lifetime chance," said Sam. "*Bon appétit, ma chère* American."

Though the elements were exactly the same as other meals, a companion, food, a restaurant that was pleasant enough, this meal was different because of Agram's declaration.

"Taste the salad. Then the meat. You'll be happy."

"Why happy?" she asked him.

"Just happy, that's it," answered Agram.

"Do you mean that food's enough to make you happy?"

"What else is there?"

"How can you possibly ask a question like that? I mean that food just isn't that important to me."

"Is the fact that I love you important? And forever," he added.

"Of course it is," she answered in a whisper. "More important than I can say."

"How important?" He squeezed her arm.

"So important I can't even begin to tell you."

"Try," said Agram. "You don't seem as though you're serious now. Are you serious?"

"What do you mean, serious?"

"Do you like me?"

"You?" she asked, needing time to gain her bearing. His announcement of love was more affecting than she could have predicted.

"About me and you," he said.

"About us?"

"What are you doing?" he said.

"I don't know."

"I do," he said. "This love is too big for you to understand."

"What about Cleo?"

"Cleo?" he said, angry. "She's not a part of this picture."

"What is the picture?"

"Only Agram el-Kassim and Melanie Markowitz eating dinner and in love."

"Have you enjoyed this meal?" asked Agram a minute later. He kissed her. "Is your mouth learning about food that isn't plastic?"

"Yes," she said.

"This is only a beginning," Agram said happily. "You don't know the rest."

"What do you have in mind for me? Can you say?"

"Of course I can say. Don't you know by now about my English?"

"I wasn't referring to language," said Melanie. "Plans," she continued. "I want to know your plans for me."

"First my mother's grape leaves."

"Your mother?" she said nervously. "Should I meet your mother?"

"No," he was emphatic. "How can you meet my mother? She would be shocked. My mother is religious. She doesn't understand your life. Of course she knows about my cigar box with all those girls. I talk to her. I tell her everything. It's seeing she doesn't want."

"How will I taste her grape leaves, then? Maybe you can make an exception in my case, and bring me there. Tell her this time the relationship is different," she said hopefully.

"I will steal them out for you. I will tell her my children want them. Later I will tell her the truth."

"Couldn't I see her as a journalist? She might have an opinion about what the Arabs here want. I'd like some exposure to the older population here, and so far I've just met Fuad's mother, who hesitates to talk to me. I have a feeling she doesn't like me at all, and I'd like to meet someone who is more impartial. If your mother doesn't know about us, she can't have any ideas in advance. Besides, it would help me to understand you. Won't you reconsider your position?"

He refused to answer her directly. "She is very intelligent. Her secret is a cracked plate," he said. "It always works."

"What does it do? When does she use it? Did she crack it herself?"

"For the grape leaves," said Agram. "That's all."

"She wraps them on it?"

"You know nothing," said Agram, impatient. "How do you expect to meet my mother? You can never understand. To try is stupid. We are a very complicated people. The plate," he said with great seriousness, "can only be on top."

"Of what?"

"Even this thing is too difficult for you. So how can you expect to know anything else?"

"Why won't you explain it all to me? I'm anxious to learn."

"That depends."

"On what?"

"On the way things develop. We are in an uncertain area. You never know on what side is buttered your bread."

"I thought Arabs don't use butter."

"That is American," said Agram. "I learned it from your famous writer Hammock."

"Hammock?"

"He writes mysteries," said Agram. "Even your own culture I am teaching you now. He was married to a Jewish girl like you. A writer. Famous over there."

"There is no Hammock."

"Many," he said. "Why don't you go to one of those schools and learn something? His wife made a movie. They showed it in Haifa with Vanessa Redgrave. She's a friend to the Arabs."

"Hammett," said Melanie. "You mean Dashiell Hammett."

"What are you doing over there?" asked Agram. "What kind of a name is Dashiell?"

"You will never admit you're wrong."

"I am not wrong," he said, annoyed at her. "Being wrong is ignorant. Are you saying I am ignorant?"

"Questioning is true intelligence. Tell me more about the plate. I still don't understand it."

"Your mind is just a book," said Agram. "Who needs books? What plate?"

"Your mother's."

"Oh, that," he said. "I told you already. It's her secret."

"How does she use it?"

"If I said it to you, it would not be a secret. You can't think that I will betray my mother." He looked upset at the idea. "It's a family secret. Passed down for generations. You are not in my family."

"I'll tell you one of ours," said Melanie. "My mother cleaned everything in the house with a tube of toothpaste. Her diamond ring. The ceramic tiles in the bathroom. The silver. But she used baking soda for her teeth."

"What is baking soda?" asked Agram.

"Would you have some of our coffee?" Sam intervened. "Or would you like to drink it American style?"

110

"What is that?"

"She doesn't know her own country. We must teach her," said Agram. "She needs to live here to learn about life."

"If you need a job, you can work in my restaurant," said Sam. "Forget about finding out information. What you don't know can't hurt you." He looked proud.

"He likes the movies too," said Agram.

"You'll learn to cook," said Sam. "You'll be happy."

"I don't know," Melanie answered. "It's not so simple. What would I tell the paper?"

"Tell them you're busy," said Sam. "You are doing research. Now, what kind of coffee do you want to drink?"

"If you wouldn't mind, could you explain what American coffee is?"

"Nes," said Sam. "You know Nes. It's all over. It's a powder from Switzerland, but they drink it in America. You put it with hot water and mix with a spoon."

"It's too quick," said Agram. "It does not taste good."

"I'll take the Nes," said Melanie. "I'd like to try it."

"Why that? Why not tea at least? With nana?"

"What is nana?"

"You mean you don't even have that?" Agram was finally exasperated.

"Menta," said Sam. "Green from the ground. But one thing they do have in America is girls with long legs. So would you like to work here? You would meet many people. Nice and friendly. It's a chance to learn the business from the bottom."

"I already have a job."

"I told you she's a journalist," said Agram.

"What kind of job is that for a girl?"

"It's a good job."

"But you're running all around in circles, for what? No home. No family. Here at least you'd learn to cook, to make a man happy."

"I'm not interested in making a man happy."

"Is she one of those?" said Sam to Agram.

"I know she isn't."

"So what is she talking?"

"You know, Sam," said Agram, "America is funny. Women wear pants."

"It's their legs," said Sam. "I told you before, they have long ones over there. I've seen them."

Fifteen

"Where is she?" Mordecai shouted to Shari at eight one Monday morning.

"Where could she be?" Shari replied.

He came unannounced the day after Agram declared love. Fuad was in the bathroom shaving with his Vetiver shaving cream from France. Melanie was lying on top of her bed, thumbing through a Zionist anthology. Shari was frying eggs in the kitchen in a Teflon pan her mother had sent her from Great Neck. The smell of burning butter was heavy in the air. Fuad's mother prayed loudly. Her voice sounded muffled and continuous. It was a saint's day.

"So where is she?" repeated Mordecai loud enough for the whole house to hear him. "Are you hiding her from me? I must see her. Or else." His voice quavered, making him sound nervous and unsure. Shari was moved.

"Don't worry. She's alone in her room," she told him, "reading about Zionism."

Melanie listened to this apprehensively. She waited, trying to imagine him stepping toward her in his soundless way. He had explained that in the army men learn to tiptoe in the desert, a difficult exercise worthy of the most agile ballerinas. They do this in case the enemy is within earshot.

"Good morning, my beauty," he said, nearly breezy. "At last I see you. Why do you break my heart?"

"What have I done?" She was sitting on top of the bedspread

113

cross-legged, still wearing her light blue nightgown. It was translucent.

"Done? Done? Done, you ask. What have you done. You tell me that answer." He sounded gentle, almost understanding.

"I don't know what you want to hear. As far as I know, I haven't done anything that is any of your concern. Why are you so upset?" She feigned innocence, guessing he'd probably heard about Agram.

"That's not what I know," he said, swaggering back on the heels of his sandals. Then he leaned forward, hands on his hips. He looked a little like a cowboy. "You have broken my heart," he repeated a little louder to make the message clear. "You did it on purpose."

"What was the purpose?"

"Destruction. Maybe you are just an evil woman, but I didn't know that. Like Delilah and Jezebel and Zsa Zsa Gabor. All you care about is ruining the men."

"What do you mean by ruining?"

"Don't pretend with me," he said sternly. "I know about you. You know you are the ruining type. We were friends, and now it is impossible because of your ruining."

"What did I do?" she said, still biding time.

"Don't pretend anymore. I am angry," he said. "You didn't show loyalty. My father was the same. She did not forgive him. Even today she is angry."

"Do you mean your mother? What did he do to her?"

"He died and left her all alone."

"Why was that his fault? He couldn't possibly have done anything about his death."

"She hates to be alone," he said. "My father knew that."

"But how could he have stayed alive?"

"Why are you taking his part? My mother's been unhappy seventeen years, and still he is dead."

"What have I done to you?" Melanie asked him. "I can see you are unreasonable when it comes to your father, but maybe you'll be more coherent with me. What's the matter?"

"You don't want to confess. You're just pretending. You know. Admit it."

"Admit what?"

"About Agram."

"What about him?"

"You tell me the story," he said meaningfully.

"I have nothing to tell you. I like him," she said. "That's all."

"Like?" he shouted. "Only like? You say that after what happened?"

"What do you want me to say?"

"Say the truth." His voice was so loud that Shari ran in, holding onto her kitchen towel.

"Tell the truth," she corrected.

"She wants to know too," said Mordecai. "So tell us. We are your friends. What is happening?"

"Nothing is happening," Melanie said quietly. She sounded innocent, detached.

"Don't try to pull cloth over our eyes," said Mordecai.

"Wool," said Shari. She sat on the edge of the bed. "I've been living with a non-English speaker for years," she added. "It's OK."

He stood up very straight and gazed down at the women as if he were standing on a ridge overlooking his troops at the beginning of a large and important battle.

"Is something going on that I don't know about?" inquired Shari. "Are you withholding information from me? You really haven't talked too much about yourself since you came." She sounded accusing.

"You can say it again," emphasized Mordecai.

Shari stood up and placed her hands on her hips like Mordecai. She pursed her lips, frowned straight into the air, and said, "I have been very honest with you," while not quite looking at Melanie.

"So have I," said Mordecai.

"I have not been dishonest."

"You have certainly not been forthcoming," Shari said. "I know nothing about your life. Or your politics," she added for emphasis.

"You see?" Mordecai addressed Shari. "She's sneaky." He winked at Shari in complicity.

"I don't know. I didn't have that impression until now. Fuad thinks she's just uninformed."

"I can prove it."

115

"Are you sure?" she answered. They ignored Melanie's presence.

"I am sure," he replied. He smiled again, suddenly and mysteriously calmer. "And how is Fuad?" he asked, solicitous. "How is the business of brides?"

"Still good," said Shari. "There continue to be a lot of weddings here, though I'm not sure why. Marriage is as profitable an industry as it ever was in Nazareth."

"I know," said Mordecai, nodding. He walked closer to Shari. Melanie watched them as though they were on stage.

"What are Fuad's plans?"

"As long as there's marriage, he'll continue to work for his uncle."

"And what about the book?"

"He writes," said Shari. "But only at odd moments. He says he's waiting for the propitious time to present his epic. Actually, though, he's a practical man."

"We all are here," said Mordecai. "It is common to this region. Don't you agree?"

"Marrying Fuad was not so practical," said Shari. "I've managed to alienate half the world."

"You married in Michigan, didn't you? There is still the other half," he answered.

"They don't care enough for it to matter."

"You can always leave and go home."

"I have been considering," said Shari slowly with the dramatic emphasis that came from a Great Neck childhood, "moving someday to Haifa. On top. Somewhere with a view down the mountain."

"A good idea," said Mordecai. "Haifa is beautiful. I have friends there."

"If neither of you minds terribly," Melanie interjected, "perhaps you could continue this discussion somewhere else. I am interested in getting dressed."

"Why bother? You'll just have to take it off again."

"What do you mean by that?"

"Do you think I was just born? Why do you continue to pretend that you do not understand me?"

116

"Because I don't."

"Should I spell it to you?"

"Go right ahead. I'm not afraid of anything you might say."

"That Palestinian," said Mordecai with a tone of voice that implied he was saying "that gorilla."

"There are a lot of them."

"A lot of them? A lot of them? You mean there is more than one?"

"Over two and a half million," she replied. "According to my statistics, there are more Palestinians worldwide than Israelis."

"What are you talking? Do you think I don't know your tricks? You think you can get away with this?"

"What tricks?"

"You are always trying to change the subject."

"I'm not sure I know what it is."

"You see, Mrs. Fuad Hassan," he said to Shari, "she's pretending. She's very good at pretending. But you know and I know."

"If you both know so much, what are you bothering me for?"

"Because I want to make sure you know we know."

"OK, OK. So what?" Melanie finally sounded angry. "Just let me get dressed."

"For what?" Mordecai asked. "To make a revolution? To destroy your own people? Just because somebody said a few nice words?"

"What words are you talking about?"

"You tell us what words," said Mordecai. "We are waiting."

Shari invited him for breakfast and they all ate together, even Fuad's mother, who was unexpectedly pleasant. "You are in the army?" she asked him in surprising English. "My brother was in the British army."

The result of all this was that Mordecai began appearing every evening at 6:30. He made a date that very morning. Because there was competition, he showed the persistence of a hungry dog. His pursuit was so rabid and determined, as if he were conquering Everest or seeking the holy grail, that every night at 6:30 Melanie would give in.

For one thing, she had nothing else to do at night, because Agram, the reason for Mordecai's sudden devotion, had not called or come by for days. He ignored her. She would walk by the cafe as if by

117

chance, seemingly unaware that he'd be sitting there, wide-legged and thirsty, and he would not even call out hello. Nothing. He ignored her for eight days. She tried reading, working, interviewing. She went to a library in Tel Aviv and looked up Palestinians in the card file. There were three drawers full of material. She read as much as she could. She sent a telegram to the newspaper saying the story was more difficult than she'd anticipated, asking for more time. She interviewed Fuad's uncle. His daughter was involved in underground politics. She interviewed an old lady who used to own a restaurant in Washington, D.C., and moved back to Nazareth at seventy-five. But all the time, she was waiting for Agram to reappear.

Of course she could have walked right up to him any one of the afternoons she walked by him and asked outright why he didn't call, if something or other was wrong. But she knew that asking spelled defeat. Once she admitted to him that she was waiting, he would consider the game won. Checkmate, without a chance for rematch. The most she could do was write a letter for the cigar box, and she wasn't yet ready for that.

Was he seeing Cleo? Even that was hard to know, for Cleo stopped talking to her too. Nathan crossed the street when he saw Melanie coming. Shari didn't know, and Fuad, if he did, was not about to say. She felt alone, useless, nearly defeated.

Mordecai would knock on the front door every night, three short raps in a row. Shari, sitting down to dinner with Fuad and his mother, would answer the door. Reserved at first, slowly growing warmer as the nights progressed, she would ask him how he was. He would always answer, "All is well," in a voice that was both hearty and high. "And how is Shari?" he would ask politely, pronouncing her name as if it weren't quite familiar yet.

"Who is it?" Fuad would call. "Who is at the door?"

"Mordecai," Shari replied every night.

"Oh," Fuad would answer, sounding surprised. He would wait for what seemed like a long time, then say simply, "Tell him to come in."

"Do come in," Shari would repeat.

118

"I am waiting here for your visitor from America," Mordecai would answer.

"Come in, come in." Fuad grew quickly impatient.

"Yes, OK." And Mordecai would enter the room, joining the rest at the dining room table.

Meanwhile, Melanie would be listening to it all from her room. When she heard him rap at the door, she would look in the mirror to assure herself that, even though she hadn't wanted him to come, she wouldn't disappoint him. She would wait, listening to the same dialogue every night, sitting like a soldier, knees locked together at the end of her bed, until Fuad called from the other room. "Your visitor is here," he'd yell out, implying that she should take the visitor somewhere else. She would jump up from the bed, check the mirror one last time, and walk out slowly, saying "Oh, hello" in as surprised a voice as possible. "What are you doing here?"

"Are you still writing the answers?" he'd ask with a smile. Then he would hand her a present: a chocolate bar in a bright red wrapper marked *Nuts* in big letters across the bar's middle, or a small paper bag of chocolate orange peels.

"Do you want to know what I'm writing?"

"Tell me later," he'd say. "I wish you would just ask me what you want to know and be finished."

"What do you think I want to know? I've told you a hundred times. Besides, you're not a Palestinian."

"Do you have to be American to listen to Elvis Presley? I'll tell you, I'll tell you," he would say and then laugh. "How about a fish? We can talk after we have some nice fish."

The Hassan family would listen intently to all of this. Melanie and Mordecai stood in front of them and talked, making no attempt to talk in private. The Hassan family, too, did not disguise their listening. They stopped eating and just watched. Sometimes they joined in.

"Tea?" said Fuad's mother.

"We'll both have some. And then we'll leave for the fish."

"Why are we drinking tea before dinner?"

"It's hot," said Mordecai. "You drink tea when it's hot."

"In America, you make a mistake," said Fuad. "All that soda. It just makes you hotter. Too sweet. We've been hot for years. Try some tea."

"They're right," said Shari. "I didn't believe it at first. Though I still wish there were some ice around. I've been thinking of asking my mother for an icemaker for our anniversary."

"It's no good for you," said Fuad. "Too cold. Ice makes you sick. Why do you think they get those colds over there?"

"What kind of fish are you thinking of having?"

"The best in the world. Saint Peter's." Fuad's mother smiled at this. "It's very famous fish," Mordecai continued. "No other fish is the same. The restaurant owner is a good friend."

"Where is the restaurant?" Melanie asked this.

"Wait, wait. You don't have to know now. We don't go until we drink the tea. The only thing we have is time. Have the tea. It will make you calm. It's good for nerves. Do you see anyone else asking questions? That's because the tea makes them easy. Drink it."

"Drink, drink," repeated Fuad's mother.

"The truth is I don't have much time," Melanie explained. "I'm under a deadline."

"It doesn't matter, even to you. And your job doesn't either."

"You're wrong. I have only nineteen days to understand the Palestinians, to know what they think, and to be able to write my report."

"No one cares," said Mordecai. "No one wants to know what Palestinians think, except maybe other Palestinians. And even they are divided, like the Jews. Maybe you can find one or two who are interested, but not many."

"I care," said Melanie. "I hadn't realized how much until I started reading. I want to be able to present their story somehow."

"Not really," said Mordecai. "If you did, you'd have written it already. The facts don't matter. Besides, you work for a newspaper that nobody reads." He said this in a matter-of-fact manner.

"We are an important voice that should be heard."

"No one is listening. The people in power know what they think without you."

"Maybe they will change their minds. Maybe the paper can help someone, even one person, to understand the difference between right and wrong."

"Do you know?" said Mordecai. "I don't think so. And when you're in a war, do you think about that when an enemy comes? Does it matter who the enemy is, whether he's right or not? Maybe to someone writing about it, safe at home and watching. But to the soldier, all that matters is his life."

"What about reason and justice?"

"Americans are the only ones who think those things exist. That is because there are no wars in America," said Mordecai.

"I would not have expected this, but I agree with him," Fuad interjected. "Not that our perspective is the same, but our philosophies are more similar than I would have guessed."

"Does that mean you both would be open to dialogue?"

"What for?" said Mordecai. "What good is talking?"

"My novel is the dialogue," said Fuad. "I'm writing it to engage the public in our saga."

"I'm not sure books are capable of doing that," Melanie said. "I'm worried that enough people won't read about your point of view."

"Stop worrying," said Mordecai. "All you have to worry is about how you want the fish. On the grill or in the pan."

"I'm not even sure I want to eat fish tonight."

"Of course you want. You want the fish, and you want me." He laughed, and so did everyone else at the table.

"Why do I want you?"

"You're a smart girl," he said. "And so, we will eat the fish and then . . ." His voice fell ominously, the gleam in his eye intensifying.

"All right," she said, hungry by then.

In the car, he would often ask, "If the Nazareth hero loves you so much, where is he? Why would he leave you alone? That is always a mistake. You don't leave the girl you love. You stay there."

She would refute this, defending independence, freedom, the right to come and go, modern relationships where coupling was mostly coincidence. But she thought he was right.

121

"Where is he?" Mordecai would ask. "What is he doing? What difference does it make anyway? He's a member of a group that wants to kill you."

"What are you talking about?"

"You know what I'm talking. I think you might know too much. Maybe you are one of them. What was your father's last name?"

"The same as mine."

"Oh, so you think you can't be tricked. Who was Joseph Trumpeldor?"

"I don't know. Who was he?"

"A great Jewish hero." He said this with a smirk, as if she'd fallen into his plot to expose her.

"So what?" she said.

"You don't know about your own people. You read only about them."

"I don't understand the we and the they. Why are you my people?"

"We are your people and that's it," he said. "It's simple."

"That makes no sense."

"Why not?"

"You're not what I want. You are football players with guns. Simple-minded soldiers with no sense of perspective, or humor. My people are Lithuanian. Some were students of the Vilna Rebbe. We studied and discussed. The women too. We wanted to learn, to exchange ideas. You're not that way here. You only care about winning. Winning is all that counts. You don't care about anything except yourself, and even that you don't understand. You are a practical people. Life is just meat and potatoes. Or a falafel and coffee."

"What about fish?" said Mordecai. "I am hungry. What's the matter with you? You don't want to eat? All of a sudden you're Twiggy. Who wants to be with a stick? You'll like the owner. He's intelligent, a scientist. You'll see ideas when he opens his mouth. For a smart girl, you really don't understand a thing." And he would put his arm on her shoulder. "So tell me something else. Forget about politics."

122

"I'll tell you what happened to me on the bus to Tel Aviv. I got on in town and the bus was already full. It was a Friday morning, and people were going for the Sabbath. An older woman, toothless, wearing a flowered scarf around her head, got on the bus with her chicken. She acted as though the chicken were her friend. She was holding him gently and talking. The bus driver didn't blink. The old woman walked to the back of the bus. As I said, it was very crowded. She sat down on the aisle, the last seat before the final row. She placed her chicken very gently next to her, giving him a window view. The whole bus was watching her and instantly started to protest.

" 'The chicken doesn't deserve a seat,' shouted a man in front. 'What will happen to the people who get on in Tivon? Get that chicken off.'

" 'And why not?' the woman exclaimed with a vehemence that seemed unlikely.

" 'Because there's no such thing!'

" 'As a chicken?' said the woman. 'Then what are you getting so upset about?'

" 'I refuse to ride on a bus where a chicken has a seat.'

" 'He's good enough to eat but not to ride?' shouted the woman.

" 'Eating is one thing. Riding is something else,' answered the man.

"The bus divided in two on this. The discussion assumed the seriousness of a border debate. I have never seen anything like it. The driver didn't move the bus. He turned around dramatically, the weight of Solomon on his shoulders. 'I have the answer,' he said slowly. 'The chicken can sit, but only on her lap.' No one protested. The lady lifted the chicken up and the bus resumed its ride. What does it mean?"

"It means," said Mordecai, "the driver is boss." He leaned over and kissed her nose.

Sixteen

It really did seem to take forever, but Agram eventually did reappear, almost as if he'd never been away.

"Where were you?" she asked him more loudly than usual. "Why did you ignore me whenever I walked by? And why did you leave in the first place?"

He was standing in the doorway of the Hassan house, early one morning. The rest of the house was still asleep, but Melanie knew it was Agram when she heard the soft, insistent knocking. She ran to answer, throwing her white terry cloth robe over her light blue flowered nightgown. She opened the door with a feeling of great relief. He looked like an immovable bulwark, standing in the early sun.

"What do you mean, left you?" said Agram innocently. He smiled at her. "I went nowhere. I did not move from the seat I have had for many years. Here I was."

"But you weren't with me."

"I was not without you either," he said cannily, then smiled. He stood closer to her then and repeated, "I was nowhere else." He placed his hand on her shoulder with force.

"That's not what matters."

"It is the only thing that matters. You were Mata Hari and Benedict Arnold."

"I don't understand how you know the things you do."

"You will never understand. You think this is the desert. We have been seeing your movies for many years. Since before you were born there was a movie house in Nazareth. Two. But one is only Indian."

"Why Indian?"

"Why do you think? Where else would the Indians have to go?"

"So you learned all you know from the movies?"

"And tradition," he said. "My people have a tradition, not like yours. Father to son."

"What are the rules?"

"I told you. Keep your eyes open and your mouth."

"Why my mouth?"

"For eating," said Agram. "It's very important here. It's the center of life. To eat. Maybe you can learn something. There are some things from life that are not in the movies."

"What are you doing here now?"

"Do you think I came to see Mr. Fuad Hassan? Don't be stupid. Hurry up. Bobby is waiting." Agram pointed outside to Bobby, smiling and sitting in the same old dusty car. "You cannot go like that," said Agram. "We are going to eat breakfast. You are not ready."

She changed quickly, and when they were eating, he handed her a package. "They are earrings," he said. "If you don't have holes, you will get them." They were beautiful earrings, a rich yellow gold. Although Melanie's ears were pierced from birth, Agram was not really aware of details, big or small, on other people. He did seem overly aware of his own facts, though, claiming to know exact things like the number of hairs in his nose.

"Where did you get them?"

"Why does it matter?"

"It matters to me. Did you buy them yesterday or a week ago?"

"What difference is it?"

"It will help me to place them somewhere, before you gave them to me. To put them in a context."

"All that's important is that I gave them to you. They're worth money," he said. "Our women wear gold, in case they have to run. That way they always have something." He bowed suddenly, then

126

bent one knee. "Take these earrings as a gift from the city of Nazareth," he said. "And your Agram."

"Which half of the city?"

"Do you think those Romanians would give you ice in the winter? I'll bet you wonder how I learned that," he said, self-satisfied.

"I know."

"You don't."

"I read it in one of your love letters."

"She was wrong," he said. "I am a very generous man. You see, I am giving you these earrings. They are genuine gold. Fourteen karats. I am giving you gold for what. For nothing. You don't have to give me anything. Though you could send me a record from Simon and Garfunkel when you get home. The one with the bridge. I will sing it. But I didn't think of that when I bought your gift. I give them to you and good luck." He breathed deeply and stood up.

"I can't accept. They are too valuable. Besides, I feel as if you're giving me these as a bribe to win me back. So that I won't be angry at you for leaving me. I've made up my mind. I can't accept."

"You have no choice. You can't say no to Agram."

"No," said Melanie, sort of afraid.

"Very funny." He laughed heartily. "You are a funny woman. Put them on already. Don't you want them? If you don't have holes, we will go to the woman with a needle."

"I told you I have them."

"I heard you," said Agram. "So why aren't they on your ears? They are called hoops in English. They look good on everybody, young or old. My mother has them."

She put them on. Agram kissed her on the side of her ear. "Nice," he said. "Very nice. Let's go for a walk so the people can see your ears."

He liked walking through town. They all knew him, everyone who passed by, and they looked at him knowingly: another one, another letter-writer from the cigar box, another woman admirer who would come and go. They seemed to approve and often smiled and said hello proudly.

"You're walking too slowly," said Agram. "What's the matter with you now? Are your ears hurting? Gold doesn't hurt like brass. It is real, I know. Maybe you're not used."

"Are we in a race?"

"Of course we are racing. We are always racing."

"What is our destination?"

"I am taking you to the man who sold me your earrings. To show him how they are in your ears. And you said you wanted to see where they came from."

"What if he doesn't like them?"

"Why not? They are beautiful. Of course he already knows that. He told me when I bought them."

"But what if he doesn't like the way they look in my ears?"

"Is there something wrong in your ears? Let me look."

"What could be wrong with my ears? They're just like anyone else's."

"Many things. Infections. Or they could be too big. Like that elephant that they put in the movie."

"Wouldn't you have noticed if something was wrong?"

"I never saw them before. And now I was only paying attention to the earrings."

"You've seen them before. You would have to be blind not to notice my ears."

"No one sees ears," he said. "Unless they are in the profession. Let's stop and look at them now." They stopped, resting against a yellowish sand wall, old and pocketed. Melanie turned her head to Agram, and he leaned over, examining the ears very seriously. "I can find nothing wrong," he said. "We can go see him now. He will be more interested in the earrings than your ears anyway. They are beautiful, and he is a businessman, so business comes first."

"What about my ears?" said Melanie, insulted now.

"I told you I can see nothing wrong."

"I'm not implying that anything is wrong. That's not the point," she said.

"Then what do you want to know? What more is there to discuss about ears?"

128

"Why don't you tell me they're beautiful?"

"Have you ever seen a beautiful ear? Look at mine," he said.

"Are they beautiful?"

"Forget yours. What do you really think of my ears?"

"They are ears," he said. "Be grateful you have them and you can hear from them too. What more do you want?"

They walked quickly to Adjami, continuing their brisk pace. Adjami owned a jewelry store. "This is the Richard Nixon of Nazareth," Agram introduced him. "Mr. Adjami was the mayor."

Adjami smiled and patted Agram on his back. "How are you today?" He winked at Melanie, then looked at her a second time. "Beautiful earrings," he said. "Why didn't you tell me they were for her?"

"I didn't know you knew her."

"He doesn't," Melanie answered nervously.

"Of course I have seen her," answered Adjami. "It is a small town here, and she is always walking. The earrings are perfect. Beautiful ears, my friend," he added seductively.

"Thanks. The earrings are beautiful too."

"We have perfected the hoop in this part of the world," said Mr. Adjami. "I have seen them in Chicago. My daughter lives there. She took me to see at Marshall Field. A very nice store. They have everything there, besides the hoops." He pronounced *Chicago* as if it were a word for a strange small insect that bites.

"Did you like the city?"

"Too cold," he said. "Too much wind. An American poet wrote a poem about it that my daughter gave me. Carl Sandburg. He's a Jewish man."

"Why do you think that he's Jewish?"

"We've known the Jewish people for many years," he said. "Even before there was a state of Israel. We have been here a very long time."

"She's Jewish," said Agram.

"It doesn't matter. We are all brothers here. Are you sure you're not Italian? Where did your grandparents live?"

"What makes you say that?"

129

"The eyes," he said. "And Italians like these hoops. They all wear them over there. I went to Italy many years ago. To look at the pictures."

"But I just got these hoops from Agram."

"And where do you think he got them?" Adjami smiled.

"Do you like the way they look on me?"

"Like? Like?" he said, suddenly angry. "It's a favorite word in America. All you Americans care about is like. What's wrong over there? By the way, I hear there's sun all the time in California. Have you been there?"

"Yes, and it is very sunny."

"Agram says you live in New York. Why do you live there? Is that where all the Jews live? It's so dirty, with nothing but crime. You can't walk on the streets, or in the big park. And there are no jobs. Even the mayor said so."

"Where did you see the mayor?"

"He came to Tel Aviv and I watched him on the news. He said there are no jobs in New York, so stay away."

"But I already have one. I'm working."

"Do you like it? How much money do you bring home after taxes? What is your line of business?"

"I work for a newspaper."

"So why do you need earrings?"

Adjami and Agram laughed at this. "Mr. Adjami is a wise man," said Agram. "He knows the way the world turns."

"So how much do you bring home after taxes per month?" persisted Adjami. "For a journalist, you don't seem to know how to answer."

"Six hundred dollars."

"Not bad for a girl," said Adjami. "How much is your rent? Do you live with your parents?"

"No," said Melanie. "Three hundred dollars. I live alone."

"You see," said Adjami. "It's no good there. In one pocket out the other."

"Not like Nazareth," said Agram. "Here we have enough."

"What about inflation?" asked Melanie.

130

"She thinks she knows," said Agram. "What's the matter? Don't you have inflation? It's all over. Not only that, you can't walk without someone putting a gun in your back. A big gun."

"At least we're not fighting a war there."

"Who says?" said Agram. "Do you believe what you read?"

"How long will you be here?" asked Adjami.

"Only a few more weeks. Not long at all."

"And how long have you been in America?"

"Twenty-eight years."

"Over here, you're an old lady," said Agram. "You should have had four or five children by now."

"You're not married?" asked Adjami. "What's the matter?"

"I married once."

"What happened?"

"We got a divorce."

"Why?" he said.

"Our lives just went in separate directions."

"In one pocket out the other," Agram repeated. "Adjami, you're right. They don't know how to live over there."

"How could that happen if you were married? What was the real problem?"

"He was a linguist," said Melanie.

"The worst," said Adjami. "You never know what they're saying because they can say anything. And what did he do for a living?"

"Languages. That's all," she said.

"Aha." He sounded knowing. "Languages. No wonder. You get paid for reading and writing in America. Everything's a business. They buy words over there. Did he love you?"

"Sometimes."

"And did you love him?"

"Sometimes."

"A marriage from heaven." Agram sounded hostile. "Go back. Write me the ending."

"You're supposed to love him all the time," said Adjami. "This sometimes business is for the parakeets."

Just then someone else entered the store: a tall woman with long hair who looked like an American intellectual. She wore large turquoise rings, and her skin was a taut suntanned brown. She was dressed in loose Indian clothes that accentuated the freedom she gave to her body: she seemed to float instead of walk, and she looked happy.

"Can I help you, young lady?" asked Adjami. "Could it be that you are looking for jewelry? What are you doing in our part of the world, might I ask you?"

"I am dancing in Haifa," she said. "For a year. I've taken a sabbatical from UCLA Berkeley with my husband, who is working for a year at the Technion doing research."

"Berkeley," said Adjami. "A most beautiful place. Very sunny. A city where freedom is emphasized above all."

"How do you know about it?" the dancer asked.

"Everyone knows about California," said Adjami. "We just discussed it today. These are my friends."

She looked around at Melanie and Agram, and smiled at them easily. "Hello," she said. "My name is Dede Figenbaum. Who are you?"

They all introduced themselves. Dede and Adjami resumed their conversation, and Melanie surveyed Agram. He was looking out the window, standing as though he were braced for what might get in his way. He looked as sure as a tree trunk or a boulder. Larger than anything she'd ever seen before, even TV wrestlers who were large for a living. So large that standing behind him was the same as standing behind a pile of sandbags in wartime. He was a man prepared for the worst, able to fight back no matter what the worst might be. When he smiled in your direction, it was as if someone were granting the right for protection: a king. Solid, tense, only sincere enough not to let that get in his way, Agram was everything that Americans, a talkative bunch, are not. His silence was a relief. Only occasionally would he break it.

"You are thinking," he said to Melanie. "Is that all you can do? You haven't even looked at your earrings from behind. Mr. Adjami, show her the mirror."

Adjami was already staring deeply into Dede's eyes. Dede looked transfixed. Agram repeated his request.

132

"Why, of course," said Adjami. "You must see how those who walk behind will see them."

"I'd like to see them too," said Dede. "What are they?"

"Earrings," said Adjami. "Stand behind Miss Markowitz. You'll get a different perspective."

"Tell them about the Israeli," Agram said suddenly. "Melanie, tell them."

"Let her drink first," Adjami said. "We must all drink." From somewhere, the same thin teenaged boy who quenched the thirst of Nazareth slipped quietly inside the door, waiting by the wall for requests.

"What will everyone have?" asked Adjami. "Some tea, or our special coffee? How about an orange drink? Or Coca-Cola? We have everything. Wonderful cakes, cookies, ice creams." He paused.

"I'll have a coffee," said Agram. "A double."

"What is double?" asked the boy shyly in English.

"I mean two."

"Two cups?"

"In one like the Americans. Twice as much. A double," he repeated. The boy seemed to approve of this. "The ladies will have the same," Adjami decided. "They are from the coasts of America, where they like our coffee very much. And some special cakes with honey. The nest of a bird, with fresh pistachio nuts and almonds, and a cream cake. I'll have American coffee. One cup."

"Now tell about the army man," said Agram. "The John Wayne. Hurry up. Tell. What are we waiting?"

"I'm waiting for the coffee," said Melanie. "I can speak better when there's something in my hand. I need to hold on."

"There's a glass," said Adjami. "A big one. I bought it for guests." He reached into a drawer and extracted a beer mug. Melanie held onto it. "There's nothing to tell," she said.

"I know already," said Adjami. "About you and Mordecai. Stay away from him. He suffers from a bad macho complex. He thinks he is king of the mountain."

"What mountain?" asked Dede. "Just for my own information."

"Mount Tabor," answered Adjami. "It's an important place for Jewish people. Are you Jewish?"

133

"I thought it didn't make any difference," said Melanie. "Why do you ask that so often?"

"It's only conversation," said Adjami. "It's like my asking are you a man or a woman."

"Wouldn't you be able to tell that?" asked Melanie.

"What a question," said Adjami. "Does it look like I can't tell?" He smiled lecherously at her.

"I have heard of an organization in the U.S. that fights for the rights of Semites," said Agram. "Is that us or just Jews?"

"I don't know," answered Melanie. "But I think it is for Jews."

"We must fight for each other," said Agram. "The world is our enemy."

"The Israelis are just puppets in the American scheme of the Middle East," said Adjami. "They are no better off than we are."

"Heavy," said Dede. "There are heavy vibes here."

"Don't worry," said Agram. "I have a solution."

"What is it?" asked Melanie.

"You will just have to wait. Patience," he told her. "I'll tell you one thing, though. Your friend Mr. Army could be in trouble."

"Why is that?"

"Because he doesn't know the future. He thinks he's going to win," said Agram.

"Win what?" asked Melanie. "And why are you so sure he isn't, anyway?"

"Look once more at the earrings," said Adjami. "I am forced to remove the mirrors. This is your final opportunity. Look, and you will know how it is for the rest of us behind you."

They all smiled. Then Agram walked Melanie home.

134

Seventeen

Letter to William Hall

What would it feel like to belong somewhere, and not belong? I keep reading poems now about lost villages: Russian or Armenian or Palestinian—losses that people can't recover. I know you think that poetry is secondary somehow, an effect and only that, but I find a certain truth in these poems. But what is it? That the people here are all the same, building a life on longing?

Americans have different problems. Most of us, except those who come from small towns far enough from big cities not to be influenced, most of us really don't belong anywhere. We are all displaced immigrants with ancestors from somewhere else. In small towns there are groups, and members of groups belonging to something: to garden clubs or Little League or Rotary. The rest of us, religious or not, are members of nothing much. The sons and daughters of foreigners, we are insecure in our citizenship, foreign in our perception of what passes itself off as a large and tolerant world. We are always outsiders. Unlike Greeks, whose allegiance is clear, or Italians or French or Africans, Americans speak a jumbled tongue—odd and childish idioms that are somehow infectious. We are imitated, our language repeated with envy and disdain in even the most remote corners of the world. Still, we are citizens of nowhere, members of nothing except a large political party whose principles were long forgotten. We do not believe, or fight, or vote in elections, or read history or speak with pride about anything much. Many of us, still young and hoping for some compelling reason for existence, wander the world in search of beauty, or lasting truths, or cultures with a larger capacity for meaningful living than our own. We are influenced by places like the Piazza Navona, but we forget even as we move on. We seem to wander aimlessly in search of gurus and perfect sunsets.

135

I have found on this trip that travelers can become instant friends. People tend to talk more honestly when there is some distance between themselves and their hometowns. I met a graduate student in art history from an ivy league college who told me a story about his aunt that he probably wouldn't have told if we met at home. She's very fat, and teaches school in a small town in upstate New York. She's been lonely most of her life until a few years ago when she discovered Italy. She's not Italian—Polish, I think—but she took a trip with the school guidance counselor and they had the time of their lives. Romance, excitement, the sort of thing she's missed before. Now every summer she goes to Italy, to the south around Naples, and this has really changed her life.

I'm sure you want me to go back to Nazareth, and what I'm finding out, but it's hard for me to relate to this impersonally. The problem in Nazareth is that it's not quite unfamiliar, yet it is. The people have become sort of Western, and they seem to be very much influenced by Western movies. Even so it remains a very foreign place.

Nazareth and all of Israel really is a cause like the UN or Marxism. Its existence, a convoluted question, is central to the lives of many, and how they define that existence depends on where they came from, what they believe. The closest most outsiders get to the life here is a brief whirl through for two weeks on a group tour. It's a hard thing to grasp.

There are others to talk to for advice about this life, journalists in the big hotels in the cities. Tel Aviv has an enormous Hilton, and Jerusalem has an old British palace called the King David. But these people seem to me to be commentators by profession, willing at the slightest hint of interest to give their opinions about anything without pausing to find out whether or not the listener agrees. Sometimes, in fact, the answer has little in common with the question. Often they seem to form opinions together, a little like art critics or painters. Journalists seem to be a pompous group, more so even than lawyers or doctors because their domain is not limited by knowledge, just proximity. They consider themselves the spokesmen for facts, for all of truth and reality. Their area of jurisdiction seems to know no limits.

Movies more than the press seems to have formed our ideas about things. In the movies, journalists, handsome men and women on screen, ruffled with a kind of down-home chic, with elegant gestures that are admirably cinematic, have nothing in common with the overweight sloppy men who carry four expensive pens of different colors in their pockets, who watch what they can without knowing the language, and write. Despite Jean Arthur and Rosalind Russell, there are almost no women journalists at all. One or two in Southeast Asia, maybe, a famous Italian who asks the kinds of questions that seem more suitable for television talk shows, a Frenchwoman or two. The newspapers we read are really from a man's point of view, not just any man's but a certain sort whose vocabulary is limited to what he can

136

type without having to look up a word in a dictionary. What I mean to say by all this is I haven't been successful in finding a journalist to help me.

All I know for sure as these days go by is that I seem to be growing increasingly confused. Soon this all will end and I'll have to say something that sounds definitive, but it isn't going to be easy, because the situation just isn't.

Melanie

"You look tired," said Shari. It was late afternoon, the sort of afternoon that happens only once in a while in some foreign countries that are not too far from a sea or an ocean. For reasons unknown, a stark white light seems to suddenly invade the day; the light holds onto objects for as long as it can, and suddenly there is darkness. It's as if the room is instantly X-rayed, revealing a secret or two, and then just as rapidly, normalcy resumes.

"Is something the matter?" Shari continued. She looked lit up by whiteness.

"It is," answered Melanie nervously. "But I'm not sure what."

Shari sat up straight in the middle of the sunshine. Even her eyebrows were glowing, and so was her face, usually pale and colorless. She was wearing a long Bedouin dress, embroidered very neatly with swirls and stars, as if the woman who stitched the design had something grandiose in mind. She looked more calm than usual, intelligent and somehow in control. "Is it the men?" she asked.

Melanie, too, looked almost beautiful. She wore a long, loose dress, light green cotton decorated with a square of pink embroidery around the neck. Her hair fell softly around her face, and her face itself seemed to have eased up somehow around the eyes. They looked more open, less peering than before. "I'm not sure," she answered quietly.

"Are you in love with either of them?" Shari persisted.

"Yes, but it's a different kind of love than I felt for my husband, or the few other men I've known in my life."

"Can you describe the way you feel? Maybe that will help."

"I don't think that they are full loves, or even quite real, but both men seem to bring out a part of me that's just willing to go along with life, that's not trying to understand or change it."

137

"What do you think that feeling comes from? Is it the men, or the place, or your article writing, or just this particular period in your life?"

"It's a very hard thing for me to say," said Melanie. "But it's something I don't want to leave. For some reason, it seems very important. I did love my husband, but our relationship was impossible because we were both trying to do the same thing in our lives. We kept getting in each other's way. With Agram and Mordecai, our lives are so different that just being together seems easier."

"Is choosing the problem?" asked Shari. "Maybe you are just too male-centered. Have you tried reading any of the important feminists like Shulamith Firestone or Robin Morgan or even Adrienne Rich? *Diving into the Wreck* might be a good place to begin."

"I've always intended to read them," said Melanie, "but haven't. How did you get these books from here?"

"I ordered them from New York. They've really helped me to understand some of my own problems."

"But what about your life with Fuad? It doesn't seem to fit in with your beliefs."

"Though I love him, I know he isn't good to me," she said. "He's really very selfish. Yael is not someone to build the future on either. Maybe I should find another job, something more meaningful. Maybe I should work with Jews. I know a little Yiddish from my grandmother. That might help with the Russians, though I certainly couldn't use it here. Do you think there are any Palestinians who know Yiddish?"

"Why do you have to work with Palestinians?"

"I suppose I don't," said Shari. "But Fuad thinks it's only right. After all, we are married, and he wants our lives to be compatible. We should be working together, not against each other. I'm not sure, though, that he really loves me."

"Would you ever leave him?"

"It is more than my mother had. She married an eye doctor," Shari answered. "My mother is not unhappy with her life, but she has no expectations."

"What about children?"

"They'd seem like strangers. How could I understand them?

They'd speak a foreign language and drink tea all day. I'd feel left out. I can't even speak the language very well. And they'd probably be ashamed of me."

"So would you ever just leave?"

"You can't. That's part of the problem."

"Why do you feel so trapped?"

"Where would I go? After Nazareth, it's hard to live anywhere else. Life is more exciting here. It's a religious center."

"But you aren't religious."

"Maybe one day I will be. Religion is one of those things that takes you by surprise. You feel it unexpectedly. If that happens, I'll be in the right place. I'm not sure what I really believe about life, but I'm glad I am here anyway. There's something about just being here."

"What do you believe?"

"My life is based on other things besides belief," said Shari. "It's practically rooted. Fuad got me out of an impossible situation. I found my life in America unbearable, and he helped me to leave."

"But didn't he put you into another impossible situation?"

"Yes," said Shari. "I suppose. But all that is changing somewhat now. There is Yael."

"Is she so different from Fuad?"

"Night and day. There really is no comparison. They seem to be at opposite ends of the universe."

"How so?"

"She's a woman, for one thing. With a different domination drive."

"Don't women dominate each other?"

"It's not the same," said Shari. "Compassion is involved."

"Do you really think Indira Gandhi is more humane? Or Golda Meir?"

"Of course it depends on the woman," said Shari. "Israeli women are a lot like their male counterparts, though the men don't recognize that. Fuad is a Palestinian man, coming from a culture where the sexes are very clearly defined as quite separate. That's an important difference."

"How do the Palestinians and the Israelis differ? It's not so easy for an outsider to tell the difference, for instance, between a Jew from an Arab country and a Palestinian. They seem closer to each other than either one is to me.''

"Can you compare an Italian with a Frenchman?'' said Shari. She seemed annoyed.

"Don't you think they are more similar than different for an American?'' Melanie said. "Especially an American who is just observing from afar, on a trip, for example. An Italian and a Frenchman wear their clothes too tight, and they seem to take themselves more seriously than we do. They hold their silverware the same way, balancing knives on the edge of their plates. Besides, they both eat food with sauces. That must mean something.'' She laughed.

"That is far too simplistic,'' said Shari. "Look at their histories.''

"Aren't they mostly Catholics, and don't they speak similar Romance languages?''

"That's like saying all Arabs are brothers,'' said Shari.

"Aren't they?''

"Of course not. Do you think the Saudis and the Syrians are similar?''

"What about Israelis and Palestinians?''

"Birds of a feather,'' said Shari. "Brothers under the skin.''

"But you said the opposite a minute ago.''

"The problem with journalists is their need for consistency,'' said Shari. "You're looking for something that can't possibly exist. It's a childish way of seeing things. There are countless sides to every question. You can choose several at once, and change your mind in a week if you like. Give yourself some room.''

As they talked, Shari made tea exactly the way Fuad's mother did. She used two different teapots, both open brass containers with spouts and long handles. Shari put a little boiling water on top of the tea leaves, then poured some of the boiling water and some of the moistened leaves together into a small glass, the kind that looks as though it's usually used for whiskey: very thin and thimble-shaped, with a gold rim around the edge. There was a lump of sugar slowly dissolving in the middle. Sometimes when she drank, she put the

140

lump right into her mouth and sucked the tea through the sugar as if to ensure sweetness, like an old woman who'd done that all her life. The tea was strong because the leaves were brewed separately from the water.

As usual, Shari served the small glasses on a tray. All objects seemed to be carried on trays: usually metal, beaten by hand into intricate designs, like Oriental rugs or elaborate sundials. They were often dark yellow, not quite golden, polished mostly, but sometimes not. Occasionally they were a soft silver gray, but that was unusual. When Shari brought out her tea, she used a tray that looked as if the pattern were an organic part of the metal, instead of imposed upon it by a hammer and tools. She would place it gently down onto a stool. There were small straw stools all over the room, hidden in corners and under tables, that slid out to hold things just barely off the ground.

"Are you saying then that Israelis and Palestinians are all the same?" asked Melanie.

"Don't quote me," Shari replied. "I am married to a man who thinks very differently."

"What does he think?"

"He thinks that one day the revolution will come and the Israelis will flee in droves to New York City and Montreal and Australia. He thinks that most of them will be just as happy somewhere else. His people, though, want to remain on this land. It's the focus of their lives."

"But what about the Jews and the Bible?" said Melanie. "And their feeling that Jerusalem is the holiest of cities?"

"I'm not sure it isn't a metaphor," said Shari. "Like Nirvana. Just a place. A place that represents peace and solidarity and freedom. Doesn't the saying 'Next year in Jerusalem' seem to mean 'Next year in peace'?"

"Maybe," said Melanie. "But somehow the idea of peace and Jerusalem seems linked. I have always connected Jerusalem with belief, and with history."

Shari explained, "It belongs to the Israelis now, and there's nothing like peace there. It's a mess, even with an energetic mayor and fancy public relations. The people hate each other. The Armenians hate the Moslems, and they both dislike Israelis. It's a beautiful place, quiet and perfect except for the people who live there. In a way it's a little like Paris.''

"But isn't Jerusalem a real holy city?'' asked Melanie. "Isn't it a holy place to millions? I have always thought it was the holiest of all cities.''

"If you mean the Wall and the Mosque,'' said Shari, "that has become an example of male commercialism in the worst way. Even Fuad says so. The believers have to work around the commercial exploitation.''

"What about Zionism? And the rights of the Jews to have a state? And the enormous problem of anti-Semitism all over the world?''

"Has Israel helped that?'' asked Shari. "The Russian Jews, for instance, just want to go to America. They want to live in Queens, like all the other immigrants. And why shouldn't they? Life is better in Queens. Zionism hasn't solved the Jewish question, it's created another set of problems. The Jews never needed a state before. Why now?''

"What about the Holocaust? It seems to me that Israel's existence is crucial for psychological reasons. Without Israel, the Jews would be vulnerable to everything.''

"They still are,'' said Shari. "Maybe even more so.''

"Why do you say 'they'? Are you no longer Jewish?''

"I actually feel more Jewish here with Fuad's family than I would if I were living in the Jewish section on top with the immigrants, or than I did with my family in Great Neck,'' she said. "You're the most Jewish of all with outsiders. Of course I am Jewish. I used 'they' to refer to others who are Jewish in different ways. There are as many ways to be Jewish as there are Jews. You know that.''

"What's Jewish about your life?''

"For one thing, I live in the ancient homeland. This is the place where Judaism originated. Great Neck has nothing to do with Jewishness, except that modern-day Judaism may have stopped there. It's a pastiche of cultural norms, not religion.''

"So you're saying that this place really does matter to you,'' said

Melanie. "And what about your marriage? Do you see that as negating your heritage?"

"Of course not," said Shari. "I am no less Jewish for marrying Fuad. Maybe more so. Contrast creates emphasis. Don't you feel more white in Harlem than you do in most other places? Does that mean you are more white there, or less? It's a ridiculous way of thinking."

Melanie looked confused, so Shari changed the subject. "Who is coming to see you tonight?"

"They will both arrive at once. I thought it was time they really did meet each other. I've been thinking about this for some days now. They claim to know one another, but I'm not sure. For some reason, I am eager to see them together, though I don't know why."

"Do you think they'll get along?"

"Not really. In a lot of ways they are too much alike."

"Can you predict the winner?"

"Now that," she said nervously, "is a difficult question to answer."

"Who would you put your money on?"

"Fortunately that's not a problem." Melanie laughed. "I have almost none."

"Personally, I'd bet on Mordecai," said Shari. "Israelis are victor types."

"I think I'll get ready," said Melanie. "I need a little time to think this through. Maybe I'll write a letter to the paper. It's seemed to help me clarify things before."

She went to her room and instantly lay down on her bed, grabbing a pen and a notebook.

Dear William Hall and the Others,

It's been a confusing time for me here. Staying and leaving are my only options, though I never realized when I began this assignment that to stay here was even remotely possible. Now I see that it is.

Everyone seems like an outsider, though maybe that is just illusion and the contrary is true. Some places have mystery, along with their birds and flags and flowers, and choosing the place is choosing the mystery, even knowing all the while that it might be nothing more than an illusion, a trick, a rabbit and a hat, an optical miracle like a pencil stuck in a glass of water that seems to bend. For me it's hard to avoid the pull of the tarot, the woman with a look that connects her to palms and answers, the possibility that just maybe, something might be explained.

Some people seem to choose clarity above all. They pick black-and-white professions: medicine, journalism, the letter of the law—disciplines with answers, with definite rights and wrongs. Others seem to have visions and dreams. They paint or sculpt, and spend a part of their days wandering. Those of us lost between reason and magic are never sure which way to go. Either path seems possible. Though magic is more appealing than law, there is something to be said for having answers. I am only able to love a dreamer, the kind of man whose relationship to facts is nonserious, who knows nothing about geometric proofs or the mechanics of a car. It's odd maybe that I have chosen to be a journalist and write these weeks about what an entire people is thinking. Circumstances dictate many things, I suppose, and few careers are based on dreaming. Maybe it would be possible to do both things: to work and to dream, here in Nazareth. Facts seem so negligible. The societies create their own truths, and that must be an easier way to live.

Journalism, now that I've had some weeks to test it differently than before (compiling facts at home is not the same as being somewhere, trying to make sense out of a place), is unsatisfying in the end. The interesting details are supposed to be eliminated from the story: the way a staple is fastened to a page, vertical instead of horizontal, or the way hairs appear on certain kinds of faces at random and unexpected points, even the pitch of a voice; these are considered subjective, and so invalid. In fact, I think they are the only story.

What do the facts ever matter? Bodies killed, official reasons why, victories lost and gained. History is usually a dull collection of facts compiled by a clerk with no imagination. What happened between the important events? Who were the people whose lives did nothing to change the world, the people who'd never heard of Marx or Freud or Einstein? They disappear in history as if they never even existed.

I feel myself changing here, as if suddenly I have to break from the track and run elsewhere. The only question is where.

Melanie

Eighteen

Melanie had imagined the meeting between Mordecai and Agram many times. They would be like Nixon and Mao, or Meyer Lansky and Al Capone, two men shaking hands and then heading into corners to fight. Civilized, assured, each convinced that theirs was the only solution, the only victory.

"That friend of yours," Agram had said late one night, "does he know anything about America?"

"Only what he's seen in the movies."

"So he's not an intellectual. A simple man, you'd call him."

"Not exactly."

"What does he know?"

"I'm not sure. I don't know quite how to describe him."

And Mordecai was just as nervous. "That friend you know," he would begin, "what makes you like him? Does he tell funny jokes?"

"No," said Melanie. "But neither do you."

"At least I know. Does he?" said Mordecai with unusual humility.

"I don't think so. If you know that, why don't you do something about it?"

"I bought a book of jokes for Americans in Tel Aviv. They are stupid. Is laughing so important?"

"If it's not important, why do you ask if he has a sense of humor?"

"Information doesn't hurt," he said.

She'd asked Mordecai and Agram to meet her Tuesday night at

145

seven o'clock. Tuesday seemed inauspicious, unlike Monday or Wednesday or weekends. She hoped to lessen the odds of calamity.

"What will they do when they get here?" Fuad asked.

"They can entertain themselves. I'm sure they'll have a lot to discuss. They seem to have similar interests." Shari was supportive.

"What?" said Fuad. "Nothing in common, those two. Black and white."

"Which one is black?" asked Shari.

"They're entirely different." Fuad ignored her. "One's in the army, the other works with wood. They have virtually nothing in common."

"Don't revolutionaries see beyond economic realities?"

"It depends on the revolution he's making."

"And she," said Shari. "What about Emma Goldman?"

"You and your Emma Goldman."

"I've never discussed her with you."

"But you think about her constantly. She was not like you in any way, yet you insist on identifying with her for inexplicable reasons."

"Why explain my relationship with her to you? It would be a waste of my time."

"My whole life is revolution," said Fuad. "And yours? Frivolities. What have you done for the struggle?"

"What struggle?"

"You see," Fuad said accusingly. "You don't even know what the sides are. Friends and enemies are all the same to you."

"Aren't they all just people?" asked Melanie. "Isn't which side you're on often circumstantial?"

"It's a matter of belief."

"But I thought you were anti-belief."

"In the unthinking sense," said Fuad. "Not metaphysically."

"How would you define your side?" asked Shari. "I was never clear."

"I," said Fuad holding his breath and then exhaling slowly for dramatic effect, "I am on your side. I am your only true friend in life. I am also"—here he paused and shut his eyes, then opened them— "your only true enemy." He looked her in the eyes, reached out for

146

her hand, and they stared at each other intensely, ignoring Melanie.
Fuad's mother was apprehensive about the meeting too. "May
Jesus help you, young girl," she said.
"Jesus will not be of much help in my case," said Melanie.
"Maybe," she said. "Maybe I will pray for you, maybe I will
not." She clung to a set of rosaries and started counting, like a Greek
man playing with his beads. "I will give you tea. Tea helps."

Everyone was ready for the guests. Even Fuad's mother had
changed out of her slippers into black leather walking shoes with
laces. She had removed her apron and tightened her bun. She looked
curious and stood in the kitchen doorway, silently waiting, hands
clasped together. Mordecai came first, beaming with the radiance of
power, soap and water, and physical strength. His handshake, a
carefully conceived ploy to prevent strangers from knowing the
truth, was faint. He did not clasp hands; rather he rested his own into
another's, as though he were weak and tired, his private joke.
"*Shalom,*" he said softly as he entered, a suitor coming to call.
"*Shalom* yourself," said Shari, smiling at Mordecai.
"*Salaam aleykum* and how are you doing?" asked Fuad, pleasant.
He tapped Mordecai's back in a friendly manner. Shari extended her
hand, but withdrew it quickly when she felt Mordecai's peculiar
response.
"Hello, Mordecai," said Melanie shyly. She ran her fingers
through her hair nervously, pushing one side behind her ear to show
off her hoop earrings, then realized her error and replaced the hair.
Fuad's mother silently waved hello from the doorway. Mordecai did
the same.
"How's the marriage business?" he asked Fuad.
"Could be better," said Fuad, shrugging his shoulders and sigh-
ing. "Though I really can't complain. My uncle, as you know, is a
very wealthy man. He got that way through weddings."
"What about the revolution?"
"It could be better," said Fuad. "This isn't my year. But I haven't
given up on either front. I am learning patience." He smiled.
"I heard on the news today that the Chinese call this the year of flat

147

fish," Mordecai reported. "Maybe the flat fish don't like you."

"It's possible," said Fuad. "We may have no flat fish here. I am unfamiliar with the species. Do they exist in Michigan, Shari?"

"I don't know much about fish," said Shari.

"Do you think the current situation is better or worse than it was a month ago?" asked Melanie.

"Hard to say," said Mordecai. "That is not the kind of information I'm allowed to discuss."

"What is your actual job in the military?" said Fuad. "Can you tell us?"

"Military jobs are all confidential," said Mordecai. "You know that."

"But some people are guards and others are spies," said Fuad. "Which are you?"

"Would I tell you if I were either one?" answered Mordecai.

Agram knocked loudly on the closed door, then opened it himself and walked in. "You are ready for me to come," he said. "I heard an American joke today about a stupid person who throws his clock from the window. The question is why does the stupid person throw his clock away? What is the answer?"

"To stop time," said Fuad quickly.

"No," Agram was smug. "Does anyone else know?"

"This joke rings a bell," said Shari.

"Wrong," said Agram. "No bells. Do you surrender?"

"Yes," the room agreed.

"I think it was in my American joke book," said Mordecai. "But I didn't memorize the answers. Just the jokes."

"To see the time go flying. A stupid person threw away the clock to see the time go flying."

"I think that's it," said Mordecai. "But I'm not sure." He laughed slightly.

"Not bad," said Fuad. "Not bad. I heard it in Michigan, maybe. Shari, do you remember?"

Melanie smiled. "Who told you that joke?"

"A teacher of grade two from Wyoming," said Agram. "We met near the bus yesterday." He leaned over to Mordecai. "I'm Agram.

148

You know me.'' He embraced Mordecai, taking Mordecai's body to his own; then he stood back, extended his hand, and gave Mordecai a soul shake, ignoring the limpness until Mordecai responded.

"Long time no see," said Fuad. "Not since the dinner." Fuad walked to Agram, and they hugged each other.

"*Salaam aleykum,*" said Shari.

"*Shalom, shalom,*" he answered congenially.

Melanie smiled up at him. "Hello, Agram," she said. "How are you?" she whispered and stepped back.

"Thank you," he replied, as if that were answer enough. One of his eyes stared at her.

"Agram, Mordecai," said Fuad. "You two certainly know each other from the vicinity."

"Of course, certainly," replied Mordecai. "We are old acquaintances."

"Brothers," said Agram, not to be outdone. "Neighbors. Why would I hate the Israelis?" he asked as though the question had suddenly surfaced. "They are my brothers. You fight with your brother, but you don't hate him. The mother is the same for both of you. When the Israelis are living downstairs and my family is on the top in the big white villas, it will still be the same. We will still be brothers."

"Amen," said Fuad.

Agram seemed nervous and was sweating as he spoke. Even his eyes looked a watery blue, and the top of his head, where the hair was thinning, beamed with moisture. "Why would I hate Israelis?" he repeated. "We are Semites. We speak the same language."

"Not exactly," said Shari. Everyone ignored her.

"And how is business?" Mordecai asked.

Agram answered him, "Today they ask for letter openers and key chains. A few years ago, they all wanted bookmarks. Now it is for keys. Everything is locked over there. The key chains go like crazy. Camels especially. The tourists all like camels, especially the ladies. My stand is famous for the best wooden camels in the Middle East. The big shops in Jerusalem all buy them from me, from charms for the pocket to a handmade camel chandelier."

"Your camels are excellent," said Mordecai. "I have seen them all over Israel."

"The wedding business is made up exclusively of brides," Fuad said. "Not everyone becomes a bride, though. You can spot the ones who will a mile away."

"Why else would they be coming into your store?" asked Shari.

"What I mean to say is that they're apolitical for the most part,"said Fuad. "Not a Marxist among them."

"Would the Marxists want a white lace wedding gown?"

"And why not?" said Fuad. "Marx had daughters."

"Beautiful dresses," said Agram. "People come from everywhere for those dresses. Americans too. You'd be surprised."

"And how are you?" Agram whispered to Melanie, meaningfully. The room was silent.

"Yes, how are you?" asked Mordecai, not to be outdone in concern. "How are you feeling?" he added.

"Quite well, thank you," Melanie said stiffly.

"And how is your article coming?" asked Mordecai.

"Thank you, well enough."

"What will you be concluding about us?" Fuad asked this question seriously. "I've wondered about that since you began the assignment."

"What do you think I should conclude?"

"The American method," said Fuad. "A question with a question."

"The Jewish way," said Mordecai. "You should meet my mother if you want to hear questions."

"No wonder you got your own country," said Fuad. "You don't stop. Just keep going no matter what. One right after the other. It's a combative technique."

"Are you saying that we Palestinians don't know how to ask questions?" Agram seemed defensive.

"Not exactly."

"Then what?"

"There's a relationship between questions and powers. In a soci-

150

ety with questions, there is trouble. There are too many questions allowed here by the wrong people."

"Don't your perfect Chinese ask questions?" asked Shari.

"The Chinese are accepting by nature. They understand, since Confucius. He spoke and others listened. They've had centuries of silence. Sometimes I wish I could live in a house where silence had a value. My mother understands that," he said meaningfully.

"Why did you study philosophy then, if you're so interested in peace of mind? Why not become a Buddhist instead of a revolutionary? Isn't philosophy the science of questions and answers?"

"They all are," replied Fuad. "Every true discipline is questions and answers. The teacher answers, the students ask. What's the difference what you study?"

"That's a very uncreative way to learn," said Shari. "The implication is that students can't bring anything to a class. Something must have drawn you to the philosophic process," she said. "Philosophy at its finest is pure questioning of truths and values."

"You're thinking of Socrates, but some of the famous Germans didn't question: they answered," he said. "They didn't have to ask. I would classify myself with them. Where's the tea?"

"Where it always is. In the kitchen," answered Shari.

Fuad spoke loudly in Arabic. Moments later, his mother appeared, laden with cakes. She seemed to slip into the center of the room, placing her dish on a folding TV table. She slid out again and returned with a pot of tea and glasses and sugar, carefully balanced. She handed a tea glass to everyone, then left and came back with a large painted bowl of perfect-looking fruit. For the first time, Fuad's mother seemed to smile very slightly. So slightly that a stranger who had never seen her normal expression would not recognize the smile for what it was. But the shape of her eyes did change, implying that her life may have been happier once. She might have smiled many times in the past.

For a woman who was fat and dark, she had an unusually graceful and mysterious manner. She could turn herself into a shadow, almost praying into invisibility. And then she could emerge again with an odd forcefulness. "Thank you," everyone said to her, and she almost smiled again and returned to the kitchen. The guests seemed pleased with the food. They ate it at once, fruit and cakes and tea, as if they were intensely hungry.

"A nice night," said Shari on several occasions. "I can feel a cool breeze, despite its being summer."

"It is nice, isn't it," Fuad would answer.

The topics were general: seasons of the year, the cost of a stereo in Germany, in Japan, in America, the poverty of India. Conversation skirted the matters at hand. The brandy was reached without incident.

"We will all drink this," said Fuad.

"What about those who don't like brandy?" asked Shari.

"Who could possibly reject an offer? This was duty-free, the finest in the shop."

"Maybe someone would prefer Sanka."

"Only Americans who don't know any better drink that."

"I will have brandy," said Mordecai.

"What kind is it?" asked Agram. "From America?"

"The best there is," said Fuad. "It's French. We got it at the airport for special occasions. Tonight certainly qualifies as that."

"I am here every night," said Mordecai. "You have never offered me brandy before. Why now?"

"What are you here for?" asked Agram. "What do you mean, every night?"

"I come on business," replied Mordecai, smiling.

"Monkey business," said Agram.

"A good joke," said Mordecai. "Business like the monkeys."

"I heard it often in Michigan," Fuad explained. "The professors would beseech us to stop our monkey business and get on with more important matters."

"You must have misunderstood them," said Shari. "That wouldn't be a very good use for that particular idiom."

"Where else could I have heard it? Why would I be so familiar with the phrase if I hadn't heard it there?"

"You just pick up things easily without really understanding

152

them," said Shari. "It's no big deal. You hear and repeat. There are plenty of people with that capability. Even parrots can do it."

"Not many people use foreign idioms easily, you must admit that."

"It depends on the phrase," said Shari. "Everyone know how to use *hors d'oeuvres,* for instance."

"That's not an idiom. It's just an accepted term in several languages."

"Words, idioms, you're splitting hairs."

"It's been very pleasant," said Mordecai. "I will see you tomorrow, Melanie. In the evening."

"I will see you in the morning," said Agram. "Good night."

And so the next week continued in just that way, with Agram arriving every day before breakfast and Mordecai returning at six every night. Lunch was the only meal she ate alone. In between visits, Melanie would go somewhere to talk or read or do an interview. At first, getting used to the idea of two lovers was difficult. She wasn't sure how she should feel, or even how she did feel. She would waver between them, sometimes preferring one to the other, usually feeling compelled to make a choice. After the meeting, neither man asked much about his competition. Each acted as though he were the only one. Agram would take her to Samir's hotel, always to the same room there, and slowly, taking his time with her, he would make love. Mordecai was less predictable about places, but more steadfast in his method. He'd whistle softly, overtaking her quickly in the car, or on the side of the road, or in ancient caves along a hillside, or even once in a restaurant ladies' room. He was a rapid lover who didn't believe in wasting his time.

"We will get married and live in Tiberias or maybe Eilat," Mordecai said often. "Water is good for you. Have you ever been to Eilat? It's very hot there."

"I went once on my group tour a few years ago. We visited a semiprecious stone factory, where I bought a green pendant in silver for my mother. It looked deserted. Is it?"

"One day it will be even bigger than Netanya," he said. "Do you know Netanya?"

"Not really. I passed through on a bus."

"It's the same as Miami Beach. Eilat will be bigger than Miami Beach."

"Are you sure? It seems unlikely."

"Wait. What's your hurry? Did you see Tel Aviv fifteen years ago? Nothing. Now look. It's like New York. Eilat will be the same. You need more patience to live here," he said.

"You will stay in Nazareth," Agram told her. "I will find you a house. You can have a job on the Arabic newspaper. The editor speaks very good English."

"But I don't read or write Arabic," she said.

"Why are you worrying? I will help you."

Nineteen

Telegram from the newspaper to Melanie:

WHAT IS GOING ON THERE? REPLY IMMEDIATELY.

Her reply:

I DON'T KNOW YET. LETTER FOLLOWS.

Later, she wrote:

I understand your concern about me and I am grateful. What is going on is simply that I am sort of in love and having a difficult time trying to decide what my next step should be. Both men have their virtues.

It's an unromantic idea maybe, but I think it's true that choosing a man to love has a lot to do with context. In outdoor settings, for instance, a man with hairy arms and legs who seems capable of hiking is at his most desirable. On bookish occasions, like poetry readings or literary panels, the paler the man, the better his chances. Women, too, are just as much victims of place and circumstance. Some countries admire large hips, feeling that only those who are so endowed are capable of true beauty and passion. Other countries hold precisely the opposite to be true. (The worst fate is to live in a place where the standards shift rapidly and unpredictably so that a broad-shouldered woman, for instance, connotes stylish sophistication one year, yet is overathletic the next.) Most of us can't help being influenced by all of this. We love different types at different stages, hoping that when we make those decisions that are intended to last for a lifetime, we are making them for reasons of substance, not whim. Everything considered, though, there seem to be no infallible reasons for choosing a partner. Because he might resemble a favorite aunt or uncle or because he plays backgammon well is as good a measure as any.

Some experts say that understanding, warmth, and compassion are the

155

qualities to seek: it seems easier to find them in a household pet. I think it has to be whim in the end, and chance.

I married my first husband for good reasons, I thought. We were both in school, both interested in ideas and in travel. But it didn't seem to matter. We were constantly competing, afraid we would somehow outdistance each other.

We fall in love, I think, with painters in Paris, or serious leftists who can argue their beliefs convincingly; with filmmakers and sculptors in Milan; with graceful men on Greek islands who can folk-dance; with holders of ancient wisdom and seekers of truth in India or Tibet; with doctors and lawyers and manufacturers in America; with Middle Easterners of uncertain professions who like soft foods and poems about trees.

I know all this, and still I find that making a choice is impossible. The options we're given often seem too close to each other, with only a hairline of difference between them. I don't know what I'll do, but don't worry. I won't forget to keep you informed.

Melanie

Asking for advice is usually a futile exercise because it is easy to predict in advance what the advice is bound to be. There are those who are willing to agree with any point of view, and there are others who are always eager to take the opposing side. When someone says they're going to get good advice, they usually mean that they're going to seek out the friend who is ready to agree with them.

For Melanie, seeking advice wasn't easy because the people she knew had too large a stake in her decision. Despite her own vested interest, however, Cleo seemed like the best person to ask just because she'd made so many decisions of her own. Melanie felt that Cleo had an instinctual understanding of things, so decided to go and ask what Cleo thought Melanie's next moves should be.

She wrote a note saying that she'd like to visit the next afternoon, and brought it herself to Cleo's apartment, slipping it under her door. Then she walked through Lower Nazareth, trying to look at the city as if for the very first time.

It was an odd place, difficult to see at first because the smells of urine and spices and coffee were so strong that it was hard to focus on anything but that until you got used to them. The streets were cobblestone, irregular clumps of rocks, some smooth and some not, that went upward into the hills of the town and broke off at random, turning into dusty dead-ends with houses randomly interspersed along the way between leather shops and hand-blown glass. The sidewalks were narrow, and it was easier to walk on the road, avoiding the cars and standing aside for the animals. Melanie headed for a nunnery on the side of a hill, figuring that maybe she could interview someone when she got there. It looked like a peaceful place, somewhat removed from the rest of the town and dead-quiet. Because of what happened there once, or maybe even for other, more incidental reasons, there were a lot of nuns in Nazareth, the kind of nuns who seemed not yet to have heard about Second Vatican Council. They were long white nuns, well-pressed flowerlike women from another era. They were like ballet dancers, graceful and quiet, soundlessly moving through their gardens behind high stone walls. It was hard to see them head on: they generally seemed to be standing sideways, their faces hidden by the whiteness of their clothes. They were as important to Nazareth as anything else, like delicate edges of lace around the city borders. Their churches were often the subjects of picture postcards, the kind that one-eyed men sell in front of holy sites. The postcards rarely had the nuns themselves in them, though sometimes, on rare occasions, when the picture-taker had been careful, a nun was caught inside a window, or even picking flowers. Generally, though, they resisted having their pictures taken, like Mayan Indians or Orthodox Jews.

It was a religious city at best and at worst. Churches were scattered everywhere, along with men in brown dresses who claimed to be close to the heavens. There were mounds of frankincense and myrrh in wooden barrels throughout the marketplace. The brown-dressed men sunbathed along the hillside in the summer. It was all a part of life, the way baseball is around famous stadiums. The townspeople took it all for granted, really. They didn't even notice that God is a business, the sort of business where postcards play an important role: pictures of holy sites that pilgrims can send to each other.

It was hard to be in Nazareth and miss the religion, though of course there were those who saw only other things: animal lovers, for instance, tended to concentrate on stray cats or the too-thin camels. Even so, the religion was difficult to miss. Though it wasn't so obvious as in Jerusalem, for instance, or Bethlehem, even so it was very much there.

The nuns were reluctant to be interviewed, though Melanie had written twice asking for an audience. She decided to approach the convent herself, just to see. From afar, they seemed like beatific and difficult subjects who smiled more than talked. They were cleaning the afternoon she arrived, scrubbing the floors and even the walls of the courtyard.

The reception room was cool and dark. A nun in white sat at a large oak desk. She was pleasant, and formal. "Yes?" she asked in French. "Do you have an appointment?"

"I've tried unsuccessfully to make one here, and now I'm leaving the area," said Melanie. "Would it be possible to speak with someone today?"

"But of course," said the nun. "You must see Sister Theresa. She is the public relations director for us." She led her down a long, dark hall right away.

Sister Theresa greeted her regally. She was unusually tall, with a broad, very white face and luminous eyes. *"Français?"* she asked. *"Anglais? Deutsch?"* Melanie identified herself, and the subject of her article.

"We know one thing about the Palestinians," said Sister Theresa in flawless English. "We know that they are surely the children of God. Especially the Palestinians who are Christian. There are many here."

"What about the Jews?" Melanie asked her.

"We are all God's children," she replied. "Even you."

"Amen," said another sister who sat quietly in the corner of the room.

"Are the Jews somewhat lesser because they are Jews?"

"The Pope has forgiven them," said Sister Theresa. "That is good enough for us."

"For what has he forgiven them?"

"We don't speak of this." She blushed.

"What do the Palestinians think of their plight?"

"They think that God is in the heavens and all is right with the world," said Sister Theresa. She folded her hands on top of her desk.

"But what about the problems between Palestinians and Israelis?"

"God has no favorite sides," she answered in carefully enunciated English. "You can quote me word for word on that. What is your own particular heritage?" she asked.

"Why do you ask?"

"Out of politeness and curiosity," she answered. "We pay serious attention to manners here as well. It means a great deal to us to observe the forms of behavior that the secular world calls etiquette. We have a reference shelf on manners in our library. It is quite an extensive library, which includes all of the titles of Jane Austen. My favorite is *Emma*," she said, smiling.

"What else do you have there?"

"Thomas Aquinas, of course," she replied. "And a young man named Merton from your country. He has quite a following among us. We are not supposed to read him, but we do. It is one of our forbidden pleasures that we allow ourselves. Please do not tell your readership." She smiled again.

"What is your perception of the internal situation here, and the role of the church in the struggle?"

"I direct you to our office of public information in Jerusalem," she said. "Or France, if you like, where the order originates. In Jerusalem, you can speak to Sister Marie-Claire. She has written a brochure for the World Board in Geneva, explaining both peace and Christianity."

"Can you summarize the brochure?"

"I wouldn't presume to do so."

"I am Jewish," Melanie told her. "From New York."

"A Hebrew," she said, smiling kindly. "I thought so. You Hebrews are a very curious people. Intelligent, many of you, with an ear for languages. Maybe that is because of all your travel. No wonder you do well in foreign lands. I thank you, my friend," said Sister Theresa. She stood up, smoothed her habit, and shook hands regally.

The nuns were timeless people. They stood in the shadows of the olive trees, barely comprehending their role in the landscape. They did not waiver in their personal steadfastness. Like the Israelis or the

Arabs or even the cactus alongside the road, they remained true to their small plots of land. Clean and kind, they walked into and out of cool dark rooms, churches mostly, all in the name of something higher than they, something they couldn't quite understand. They were not so much shy as graceful, speaking in dulcet tones, knowing as many languages as they could. More learned than most others in the area, they were given respect because of their role with God, and because of course they are virgins.

Melanie got home comforted in an odd way by her walk and the visit. She found a note on her dresser, written in perfumed purple ink. It was from Cleo. The note said, "I will await your three P.M. visit tomorrow. Yours sincerely, Cleo Joan Ginzburg."

Melanie looked for Cleo every morning when she walked through the curved yellow streets. She would walk, hoping to find an answer to the day, or the city, or anything, walking in circles through the maze. The streets were unpredictable, easy to forget from one day to the next because they seemed to intersect at random. Even the store owners seemed to shift around, visiting each other's shops with an ease that was disconcerting.

Cleo was sometimes with Nathan, not in the way that strangers walk together, or even friends. Their steps were out of sync. They would collide as if they were walking toward each other from afar. Then they'd separate too quickly, only to collide again soon. They would see Melanie, or at least Cleo would, because she was the kind who saw everything. She would look Indian or African or even Palestinian, the liberated sort with American dress and blackened smudges around her eyes, and she would avert her eyes when Melanie tried to provoke them to recognition. Nathan would act as a shield, standing in front of Cleo on occasion, as if to protect her from the dangers of the city.

Melanie felt bad about not seeing Cleo and wanted this to change. She thought Cleo was an unusually interesting woman, maybe even more than Agram, because she didn't have to stay in one place to be what she was. She seemed to move from circumstance to circumstance with a seeming fearlessness, and she was able to absorb it all, to become bigger from it instead of diminished by the difficulties

160

involved. She was even beautiful the way a chameleon is, changing right in front of you.

In some ways, Melanie thought that Cleo had a lot in common with Agram. He hadn't married over and over, but he did at least have a cigar box and more memories from three months of sitting at his stand than most people can accrue in a lifetime. As for Cleo, when she wasn't around it was easy to imagine what it would be like if she were. Seeing her once created a void for all the times when she was somewhere else.

Melanie wanted to write to William Hall about Cleo, but wondered if he would think the whole matter irrelevant.

Shari asked what the note said. Melanie didn't want Shari to know she'd planned on going elsewhere for advice.

"It's a social meeting," said Melanie, mumbling. She twisted a lock of her hair with her finger.

"I thought she was angry."

"No," she lied. "We just haven't met in a while."

That night she prepared to meet Mordecai with unusual care, feeling that the next day's visit had the potential to influence her relationship with him forever. She treated him gently, telling him that no matter what happened, his helping her to understand Israel would remain important for her. He reacted as though she were not feeling well, and told her that he'd be glad to bring her home early, if she liked.

"Not at all," said Melanie. "I just want to savor this night together. I may be leaving soon."

"What do you mean?" he asked. "I understood that we were getting married, and living in Tiberias or Eilat. When did you decide no?"

"I didn't," she told him. "It's just that it isn't that simple. I'm not yet sure about what I plan on doing."

"What day will you tell me?"

"Very soon," she said.

Her morning meeting with Agram was peculiar too. He was suspicious of her, refusing to go to Samir's hotel and wanting instead to drive restlessly around the Galilee hills. He pointed out tombs and holy caves with odd abandon, driving so quickly that she hardly had a chance to see anything. When he reached the Sea of Galilee, he pulled right up to the water, barreling over the grass as though it were road, and then stopped suddenly, on the water's very edge. He put his arm around her, but did not pull her close. "When would you like your house?" he asked. When she said she wasn't sure, he seemed to grow even more restless. "You are not leaving?" he said. "You don't want to return to America. Nothing is there. After you've been in such a place like this, how can you go back to all those cowboys?" He seemed uncomfortable and upset, but she couldn't extract an explanation.

"Is something the matter at home?" she asked him.

"All the country is my home," he said.

"But what about your children? Are they well?"

"Why wouldn't they be?" he replied.

She returned to the house restless herself. "Tomorrow will be better," he said. "I think so." Then he held her close to him, squeezing her tight and releasing her quickly.

She went to her room, unable to read or to write. Finally she pulled out a postcard from her notebook, a picture of a cistern poised in the middle of an abandoned hill, and she wrote to her mother: "You would enjoy it here. I know you feel that Israel is not really the place for you, and maybe it isn't, but at least it's worth a trip. There's a lot to see, and the daily life is compelling in a way, so maybe you should put it high on the agenda (above China and Peru). Love, Melanie."

Then she wrote a card to William Hall. For him, she sent a picture of Capernaum. She wrote in tiny script, wanting to tell him as much as she could.

Don't worry about me. I'm fine. So's your story. I'll know what the Palestinians think by the time I get there (if I ever get there), and if I don't arrive you'll have the prestige of your own Middle Eastern correspondent. Someone on the actual scene of wars and whatever. What's happened to me here is hard to say: I've been very affected by the intensity of the daily life, in a way that I never have been before. I don't even know why, but somehow these people, for all of their faults and narrow perspectives, seem very close to me. I feel as though I lived here in a past life, as someone's Moslem

162

mother. I can almost hear myself padding through rooms in an Arab apartment with high ceilings and a patio, wandering around on early mornings, pounding oregano and making loaves of bread. Oddly enough, I find it so easy to identify with everyone here. There's something about this place, some deep and timeless hold it has that makes me wonder what I've done until now. It's a good thing, not a bad one.

Melanie

To visit Cleo, it is necessary to prepare. Because Cleo is so much a person of oils and powders, it is important to take special care with that kind of annointing yourself. Melanie considered her options seriously. She didn't want to compete with Cleo; on the other hand, she wanted to make it clear that she was trying. She decided that American Reporter was as close as she could come to costume, so she retrieved a spiral notebook from the bottom of her travel bag, along with a felt-tip black pen. She ironed her crisp white blouse with a pocket, then she ironed her navy blue wraparound skirt. She replaced her gold hoops with tiny pearl studs, hoping they looked more official. She even wore her watch for the first time since she'd arrived. She stuck an extra pen in her blouse pocket, and felt ready.

It was exactly three when Melanie got to Cleo's. Cleo came to the door immediately, an Indian princess wearing feathers and a wampum belt. She had done her job carefully, painting selves on her exterior in such a way that you couldn't see through from one layer to the next: you had no idea really whether she'd been an African priestess the day before, or a Chinese poet, or an American teacher of high school French. Her personality, too, shifted somewhat with her costumes. She could seem humble, shy, demeaning, royal, vain, or proud. It all depended on the day.

Whoever she was, she always seemed ready to receive a guest, ready to recite her lines.

"Hello," she said with distant familiarity. "How and *salaam*. I have received your note." Then she waited, standing aside for Melanie to walk past into Cleo's dining room. The room, too, was an odd pastiche: photographs of Cleo's husbands and children were hung in a circle on the side by the dining table, and pictures of Cleo herself in costume were lined up on top of the circle, ten in a row.

163

There was Cleo as circus performer, hanging from a rope in her mouth, Cleo as classical musician wearing a long black skirt and holding a violin, Cleo as figure skater, as flamenca complete with castanets, as Nefertiti and Diana, as Elizabeth Taylor in *Butterfield Eight,* as mother with her children around her, as bride in a long white gown, and as royalty, sitting on a high-backed chair and wearing a large tiara. The room itself was soft and pink, creating the impression that the furniture was all made from feathers and velvet. It looked particularly odd inside the modern whitewashed apartment building, in a place where sharp ninety-degree angles seemed more expected. The drapes, the first Melanie had seen in Nazareth, were maroon broadcloth, making the room look intimate and giving an uncertain feel to the time of day. They sat facing each other in identical chairs with a low straw table between them.

"What really brought you to Nazareth?" Cleo asked. "What brings you to this part of the world?" she repeated.

"I'm living here temporarily on assignment. You know that," Melanie answered.

"Not quite," said Cleo. "There's something else."

"That's really why I came to see you. I'm confused about my feelings here."

"I know that," said Cleo.

"So why do you ask?"

"Formalities are very important here," she replied. "A Bedouin will continue to pour coffee until he sees you turn your cup upside down. Words don't matter. It's ritual that counts."

"So what do you think?"

"I think it's an intelligent ritual. You can't possibly fill a cup that's upside down."

"Does everyone know that they should turn over the cup?"

"Not unless they've been told," she said.

"Do the Bedouins tell you?"

"They say as little as they can."

"And if you can't figure it out?"

"Then you are forced to drink a lot of coffee," said Cleo.

"Until when?"

"Until you stand up to leave. But your leaving is improper and offensive, because you haven't officially ended your coffee drinking."

"And no one gives you a clue or some indication of what is expected?"

"Not the slightest, if they can avoid it. The only way things would be different is if you were to tell them that you were an anthropologist."

"Why would that matter?"

"Anthropologists come specifically to observe customs. You can't properly observe unless you understand what you're watching. The Bedouins especially are used to anthropologists. They come here often. Other people are supposed to feel what is expected of them instinctually. The Bedouins, like many others, feel that their customs originate from a universal instinct. You should somehow have the urge to turn the cup over."

"What about my urge toward Nazareth? What should it be?"

"Urges and advice are antithetical," said Cleo. "In fact, they go against each other."

"Could you help me anyway?"

"It's in my own best interest to tell you to leave."

"Then say that."

"I'm not sure that's quite what I want you to do, or even what I think you should be doing."

"What do you think would really be best?"

"No one else can tell you that," she said.

"Do you regret any decisions you've made in your life? You seem to have made so many."

"If I did," said Cleo, "it wouldn't really matter. I've had an interesting life. I've made love many times, and lived a lot of different ways. I feel as though I've really been living."

"Would you have been happier with one man, in one house, in one country?"

"That would have been impossible for me," she said. "And for you too. How can you have only one of anything? It's a puritanical notion, only for those with limited vision. Once you've seen the

165

possibilities, it's impossible to decide on only one, so you make temporary choices that change."

"How do you do it?"

"I made all my decisions, knowing how finite each one was, knowing how easy it was to undo what I'd done, or just to move on. The decisions themselves were incidents in my life, not conclusions. I didn't decide to marry Nathan, for instance, but I haven't decided not to either. What will happen with Nathan and me will depend a great deal on circumstance, coincidence, and Agram too. If I marry Nathan, it will be because there was a full moon, a warm wind, or just a look in his eyes."

"That's all?"

"What else is there? Once you realize that all we can do is hold on for a minute or two and then disappear, decision making becomes a lot easier."

"What would you do if you were me?"

"I'd write my story and title it 'The Palestinians Think a Lot.' Leave it at that."

"But what about Nazareth? Would you stay here, or go back to America?"

"Nazareth is just a place with a chocolate factory, a history, and some Arabs and Jews. It's no more and no less. It's really the same here as anywhere else."

"I don't think so. There's something more about it, something stronger than in other places. A pull to stay. It's a place that I find hard to leave."

"So is anywhere else, if you allow yourself to love it."

"It's harder for me, I think, because I'm absorbed by it in a way that I've never felt before."

"It's not just Erie, Pennsylvania," she said. "It is Nazareth. Many things have happened here. It is a holy city after all. Jesus came here, and a lot of others after him. Many who come here are looking."

"For what?"

"It's hard to say. I don't think they could tell you themselves. Like you, though, they want a better life than they've got, and they'll use any excuse to replace the things that are too familiar with other things that give them a sense of hope.''

"But will it make any difference to their lives?''

"Only the difference of a well-executed illusion. Some people have more ability to create and sustain than others. Some seek out possibilities. Others maintain order. The world is not so different from place to place. Techniques may vary, and humor or love might too, but it's all a question of having a roof over your head and living a daily life. I don't think you belong here,'' said Cleo. "I don't know why.''

Melanie changed the subject. "You've been married so many times, how can you tell when you've fallen in love?''

"Listen to Sarah Vaughan or Um Kul Suum,'' said Cleo. "You can hear what they feel. If you don't know, then it probably isn't love. It's something else. Something momentary.''

"But I thought you believe that all love is momentary, and that's why you're able to marry and remarry.''

"Momentary does not mean less intense,'' said Cleo. "It's all love. I didn't have to ask someone else. You're still too young,'' she said. "Although I married for the first time when I was nineteen. Maturity seems to happen later these days. Our session has come to an end,'' she said. "How and *salaam.''* She raised her hand in a gesture that was a mild sideways movement, more like a step in a water ballet than good-bye.

Twenty

"So what is the matter?" Agram asked. "I know what is wrong with you. You don't have to say."

They were sitting in his favorite cafe, the Abu Nassar. *Abu* is one of those words that everyone uses in Arabic. It means *brother*, but no one ever really translates the word. Native speakers assume that through osmosis, because it's inevitable that words like *abu* are heard all the time, the meaning will be magically conveyed. They have an onomatopoetic sense of the word, but this doesn't really work in a foreign tongue, because the sense of sounds is different.

Melanie faced Agram. The idea was that if anyone walked by of importance, he would tell her. The world continued to be filtered through him entirely, but only for friends. It was a service he performed. Agram had the same characteristics as a warm-hearted monarch. He knew his people loved him, and he accepted that love as part of his due. He deserved it. It was not hard for him to find subjects. Melanie was, for one.

"Cleo is walking by," he said. "I see her on the road. She's in front of the sandal shop, though she doesn't stop there. She seems to know we are watching."

"Will you ask her to sit with us?"

"I'm not sure that would be wise. Maybe." He paused a minute, then shouted, "Cleo." She heard him at once.

"Why, hello," she replied. Her hello was mildly British. Cleo was dressed as an Englishwoman walking to the library, carrying a bag marked *British Air*. She wore an ill-fitting navy blue suit with a white blouse and pearls. Despite the heat, she looked cool and efficient. "How are you both?" she asked. "You seem well, the two of you." Her manner was almost reserved.

"Well, hello," said Agram. "You are beautiful. A real Miss England."

"I am certainly not Miss England," said Cleo. "There's no dignity in that."

"Excuse me," said Agram. "A teacher of languages?"

"Is that the best you can do?" she asked. "Melanie, why don't you try?"

"A school mistress."

"A botanist," said Cleo.

"Well, your flowers are in very good condition," said Agram. He winked at her. "Would you like some English tea and some dry bread like they eat there? I can ask for you."

"I could possibly carve out the time," she said. She looked over at Melanie, indicating that she should leave immediately. "Are you in a terrible rush?" she said. "You're looking somewhat peaked. Perhaps it would be a good idea to lie down."

"I feel fine," she replied. "In fact, I have more time than usual today. I am nearing the end of my assignment. I am interviewing Agram for the final time."

"Haven't you done that sufficiently?" Cleo asked. "It seems to me that he's been interviewed constantly by you and many others."

"Never enough," said Agram. "Some of us are like wells. Very deep."

"I refuse all chance of interviews," said Cleo. "It's tiresome."

"Do those chances occur frequently?"

"More times than I would care to mention now."

"How has that happened? How have you managed to be approached so often?"

"The circumstances of my life are extraordinary," said Cleo. "I am a woman whose experience is worth understanding, as you yourself know, Melanie. There are many who are curious." She seemed angry. She reached into her bag, a navy leather compartment with short straps that fell from her wrist like hanging weights. It was the sort of bag that looked like it contained traveler's checks and a

170

compact. Cook's instead of American Express. She reached inside and drew out a surprising cigarette case, of a soft and beautiful silver. The case seemed as though it had been in her family for years. It looked worn and familiar. Then she reached back into her bag and withdrew a lighter.

"Where did you get a Zippo?" asked Agram, his voice full of envy. "You don't smoke."

"This isn't a Zippo," she answered. "And it has the capacity to light a cigarette even in the most violent winds. At night on the desert in winter, this lighter is able to produce successful flames."

"Who took you to the desert?" said Agram. "Will you give me the lighter?"

"You don't smoke either," she said. "And my companions are none of your business, as yours are none of mine." She glared at Melanie.

"Who gave it to you?" Agram insisted. "Do I know him? Not the skinny Indian."

"I am a woman of mystery," she said. "This proves it."

"I'll be going," said Melanie.

"It's about time," Cleo answered.

"I am a better lover," Mordecai said to her that night. He didn't seem doubtful at all. "Even when we are having sex in the car, it is good for you with me," he said.

"So what?"

"So everything," said Mordecai. "Sex is all that matters. If there was such good sex in America, the girls wouldn't come here in such a hurry."

"There is good sex in America."

"We read in the newspapers in Israel that Paul Newman is no good in bed."

"How do they know?" she asked him. "Besides, Paul Newman is only one man."

"But if he is no good, imagine the others."

"What makes you think Israeli men are so wonderful?"

"I don't think, I know," he said. "Everyone is happy, and we don't waste much time."

"So you think sex is really a waste of time."

"No," he said. "Would I do it so much if I did?" Mordecai placed his hand on hers, firm and gentle. They were sitting by the water in an Arab fish restaurant in Akko. The tables were not very well balanced: some looked as though they had only three legs. A big sign over the door said, *Only Lobster in Israel and Palestine.* "They don't know what lobster is," said Mordecai when Melanie suggested ordering it.

"Do you?"

"Do you think I would eat something like that?" he asked.

"Everything is okey dokey," he said. "Stop thinking so hard. The problem with you is you're always thinking. Enjoy yourself," he told her. "Be happy. It's easy. Watch me." He balanced three spoons on the backs of each other, then flipped one in a way that made the third land smack into his water glass. "See?" he said. "It's not so hard."

"I've got a lot to think about."

"What, for instance?" he asked. "Don't worry your little head."

"That's an insult."

"Would you rather have a big head? Do you think that's good? It doesn't look nice for a girl to have a big head."

"I don't have one," she said.

"That's why I told you not to worry your little one."

"It could mean that you are insulting my mental abilities," she said.

"What is that?" he asked. "Do you think your brain works like the car? You Americans," he said. "You people know nothing and I mean nothing. We say *efes* in Hebrew. That means nothing. Do you know that word? What's going on over there in America? You tell me."

Letter from William Hall

A reporter certainly does not fall in love. (I never have. And I don't know any of my colleagues who have either.) You have us all very worried. What is going on over there? We had a board meeting to discuss your situation

172

(dilemma?) but unfortunately we weren't well enough equipped with the facts to be able to draw a conclusion from your letters. What in the world is going on? Are you happy? (unhappy?) What do you mean about love, for God's sake? You are a reporter (writer? editor? possibly all of those). The idea of a reporter is to remain uninvolved. A reporter goes to a place and covers an event, without getting lost in the context (history? day-to-day problems?). A reporter does not wander the streets. A reporter has a clear-cut task (responsibility) to do, a little like a mechanic or a doctor. You must write down all of the sentences necessary to describe an event, with as few adjectives (descriptive notions) as possible, leaving the analysis to the reader or at the very least a professional expert. Sometimes my role is to serve as that expert. When analysis was absolutely necessary, on the Cambodia question, for instance, I did that by consulting outside sources for input (suggestions). But I would not take it upon myself to explain an entire situation. Nor would I fall in love on the job.

When you were given your assignment, the idea was that you would provide a pastiche (collage? collection?) of perspectives from the people themselves: their singular voices would add up to one collective voice that would allow the reader to understand Palestinian thinking. If that is not possible, if you find yourself too involved emotionally (are they Palestinians who are involving you?) to be able to write, then we have all agreed you should forget about it and come home. We can hold a retreat to discuss the entire thing (even the personal, if you wish) when you return. Let us know when that will be. You have already exceeded your scheduled allotment. How much can the Palestinians be thinking that it's taking you so long to write? Other people have conquered this very assignment in three or four days. I just read a piece, for instance (I didn't want to send it to you, in case it would prove to be confusing), from Frederick Fedaille in Paris. A cogent (and precise) summary, I thought. So did some of the staff, though not all. Maybe you should try to meet him. He seems to have a clear idea of the situation, without becoming personally involved.

We are behind you, no matter what. If this story doesn't somehow evolve, don't worry. We will find a way out. Maybe you can write an interesting piece about your confusion (political).

Yours, WH

Late one Thursday afternoon, between Agram and Mordecai, Melanie decided that she would walk to the bus stop outside of town and just take a bus somewhere. As usual, the day was hot and humid, but she walked along the road cheerfully, glad to be going outside of her usual borders. When she arrived at the bus stop, there was already a crowd gathered waiting. They were more festive-looking

173

than usual. The women were dressed in old-fashioned cocktail gowns, with full tulle skirts and sequins. The men, while they didn't wear suits exactly, had approximations of them on in different forms. Some wore jackets over their white shirts, others wore vests or loose overshirts. The women all wore high pointed shoes, open-toed and shining. There were a few children, cleaned and ready too. They were talking together excitedly, and when she approached them, they greeted her with warm shouts of *Shalom*. An older woman took charge. "From America?" she asked in English. *"America America,"* sang the children. *"Hi ba me-America."* "They mean you come from there," said the older woman. The crowd encircled Melanie happily. "We go to a wedding," they told her. "You come too."

She hadn't intended to go anywhere in particular, and a wedding seemed like an interesting thing to see, so she agreed readily. "Are you sure it will be all right?" she asked. "Is there room for an outsider?"

"Don't be foolish," said the older woman. "Come, come, come." "Come," repeated the children. They sang it into a song.

Just then the usual green-and-white bus pulled up to the stop, but it, too, was filled with festive riders, who all seemed as though they were going to the wedding. "Come," said the driver to Melanie. "A wedding. You will like it."

She boarded the bus eagerly, and sat beside the older woman, who explained things to her. "This bus is for the wedding," she said. "Everyone goes there."

The driver passed through two small villages, stopping at random points to pick up a few of the guests, who got on with great shouts of greeting. They were introduced to Melanie one by one by the older woman, who referred to her as "the American guest." The people, it seemed, were Jews from Iraq. They'd come from Baghdad to Israel the fifties, living in tents until they were able to regain some of the things they'd had in their lives before. "We were rich there," said the old lady. "My father was the goldsmith to the king." She showed Melanie her jewelry: golden bracelets carved by hand into delicate lacy bangles for her arms, three different rings each set with a

174

perfectly cut stone—a ruby, a diamond, and a sapphire. She even removed the rings from her ears. "My father did these for me when I was twenty-one," she said. "See how beautiful." They were very beautiful: intricate earrings that seemed like ordinary hoops from a distance, but with vines and flowers curving around them, and random blossoms, centered with bright yellow stones. "My father was a genius," said the woman. "He died when he came here. He couldn't work. No gold here then. He swept the streets in Tel Aviv. It was hard for him. His friends here swept the streets too. He never found his sense of pride."

"What was your life like?" Melanie asked.

"I was already thirty-one when I came. My father was in his eighties. I was the youngest of ten children. My mother had died long before. Israel has been very good to me. It's my home," said the woman. "I could not live in Iraq."

They rode through the most spectacular landscape that Melanie had ever seen, even more breathtaking than the hills around the Sea of Galilee. The windows of the bus were open, and the hot, warm smells of farm fields overtook the bus: it was fresh and overwhelming. "Where are we going?"

"We are taking the back way to Tiberias," she said. "The wedding is there, right on the sea. Have you seen Tiberias?"

"Many times," said Melanie. "It's a very beautiful place."

"Yes," said the old woman. "Lucky for a wedding."

"Where did you get married?"

"In my mother's mother's house," she said. "Four hundred people came. We danced for two days. My husband loved parties. I was a very young girl when I married him. Just sixteen. But I know I loved him."

"How many children did you have?"

"Fourteen, but five died when they were babies," she said. "It was difficult for babies then. Not like here, where there are many doctors."

"Are your children all here?"

"Many are on the bus," she said. "All my children except one boy who was killed in the Yom Kippur War will be at the wedding.

175

My daughter's husband's sister's girl is getting married today. We will all come."

"Will there be many people at the wedding?"

"Half of Israel," said the old woman. "We have a big family here. It's not like your Ashkenazic families. One child or two. You come to visit on the holidays. Our families still live together. We see each other all the time. Israel is a small country," she said. "We live close to each other. We like to be together. We are happy in the family." Melanie looked around, and it did seem as though everyone on the bus was engaged in conversation. The men were smoking cigarettes, sitting together and talking. They passed bottles of brandy and wine up and down the passenger seats. The driver had his own plastic glass, and occasionally he, too, would partake. Sometimes one of the men would start a song, and the rest of the bus would join in. The songs were in Arabic, unfamiliar to Melanie, but it was easy to know they were all about love. "Are you married?" asked the old woman. "Do you have a husband? Why are you here by yourself?"

"I am working for a newspaper," said Melanie. "I'm finishing a story they asked me to write about Palestinians."

"Poor people," said the woman. "No place to go."

"I was married once," said Melanie. "It didn't work out. I miss having the sense of family, though."

"Where are your parents and your brothers and sisters?"

"My father is dead," she said. "My mother lives alone in New Jersey. I live alone in New York. My sister lives alone in California. That's three thousand miles away from us so we don't see her very often."

"Why does she live so far away?"

"She likes California. She likes the weather, and the freedom. And I'm sure she even likes the distance."

"Wouldn't it be better if the three of you lived together in the same house?" asked the woman.

"We would kill each other," answered Melanie. "We would get in each other's way. We are all very different people."

"So what? One of my children is a communist, one a socialist, one a capitalist. One is a painter. They are all very different. They fight. You see they are fighting. So what? At least they are together."

176

"It's not so easy for us," said Melanie. "It feels like there's more at stake."

"Will you stay in Israel?"

"I don't know. Then I'd really be far from my family."

"Maybe they would come to live here. You could all live together," she said. "In Iraqi families, no one lives alone. We help each other. Sometimes we don't get along, but it doesn't matter."

"For some reason, that's not possible with us," said Melanie. "We like each other, but we're not able to live together. I don't know why."

"Forget everything," said the woman. "Have a good time today. A wedding is good luck for everyone."

"In America, too, a wedding is considered lucky."

"You see," she said. "Some things are the same all over the world. People are happy about marriage."

They arrived at a seaside restaurant along the Galilee, across the water from where Melanie and Mordecai had eaten. It was open decks, wooden planks in a boardwalk alongside the sea. The telephone wires were hung with paper lanterns and crepe paper flowers, large turquoise and yellow blossoms that looked almost mythic, and the tables were bright colors too: pink, green, electric-blue cloths, with big bouquets of wildflowers in the middle of all of them. A long table against the side of one wall was laden with trays and trays of food. Against the facing wall was another long table stocked with bottles and glasses and bowls of punch. The people were actively grabbing each other in an excited manner. The children ran in circles, and the adults seemed to too. Melanie did not stand alone for long. Strangers introduced themselves and invited her to come and see them. They brought her a large plate full of food and stood with her to watch as the bride and the groom, a young, smiling dark couple, married each other quickly, then embraced. The men began dancing immediately after, as the band played songs that sounded similar to the ones they'd sung on the bus. A singer grabbed the microphone, a woman in a tight white dress with long black hair, and as she started to sing, the room became very quiet. She, too, sang an Arabic love song, high pitched and poignant. "It's about a new love beginning," said the man on her right. "Can I get you a drink?"

She drank whiskey out of a paper cup, and soon she was as drunk as the rest of them, dancing with a new abandon: with one stranger after another. The music seemed to get softer, then louder; it would often become a loud and plaintive wail. Whenever the singer would go to the microphone, the room would descend into quiet.

She danced through her date with Mordecai, forgetting until it was too late to return. "How will I get home?" she asked a partner. "Someone will take you," he said. "The buses will come back. Don't worry about home. You are here now," he said.

Before she knew it, late afternoon had turned into early morning. They danced along the sea carelessly, and the night fell quickly, but there were so many lights, and it was a bright night anyway, stars and a very full moon, that it didn't matter about time, and they all just whirled together, children and grandparents alike, and the bride and the groom, sometimes dancing in the middle. Melanie had never been to a wedding like that before. She remembered her own marriage: a formal exchange of vows in a small, serene room, clasped hands and flowers that matched her dress. She wanted to do it all over again.

The bus drove her back to Nazareth, with all the same people. The children slept, but the adults continued their singing and drinking, and when Melanie walked into the house at nine o'clock in the morning, she felt elated yet calm, as though she knew her next step. Shari had left a note on the kitchen table saying, "Mordecai and Agram worried about you. They both asked that you get in touch. Where were you anyway? I'll be home by four today. Don't go anywhere." Fuad, too, had left a note. "I'm in the bridal shop if you want to come by."

Fuad's mother came out from her room when Melanie entered. She smiled at her. "Tea before you sleep," she said. Then she poured a glass of tea, gave her a small sweet cake, and disappeared again, patting her on the head first before she left the room. This was the first time Fuad's mother had ever touched her. She felt the touch for several minutes after.

The house was dark and quiet. Melanie walked slowly to her

room, taking her dress off as soon as she got there. She put perfume
behind her ears, then got naked into bed. The sheets seemed freshly
ironed, and she slid onto them, dreaming instantly. She dreamed that
she was living in an Arab house in the middle of an ancient town, a
town very much like Damascus. It was an old and beautiful place, the
golden color that comes from centuries of sunshine, golden white,
like perfect ears of corn. Luminescent almost, the way cities can be
in a dream. The house had an open courtyard, and a wall that
separated the yard from the street. No one walking by could see it.
The patio was exquisite. Rich blue painted tiles, the color of an
ancient Persian city, deep lapis decorated with gold and red and blue
designs, magical designs really, forming an intricate and harmonious
pattern that created a feeling of deep and lasting peacefulness.
Lemon trees, fragile and perfect, so fragrant they made the whole
house feel yellow and wonderful, were all around the courtyard, and
so was a stream of water, springing from somewhere within the
rocks. Birds flew easily, colorful birds that looked as though they
could glow in the dark. The place itself made Melanie happy, happy
in a way she'd never felt before. When she woke up, it was already
dark and she could hear them all walking by her door and whispering.
She told them about the dream, and how it seemed as though she
would stay, if only because she had that kind of dream.
  "Yes," said Fuad's mother. "You will stay."
  "We can teach English together if you like," offered Shari. "I'd
be glad to go into business with you. We could teach English to
anyone who wants to learn." Shari sounded optimistic, more pleased
than usual.
  "What will you tell the men?" said Fuad. "You have to tell them
something."
  "I'll see them both once more," she said. "To say good-bye, and
to let them know I am moving away from Nazareth. There's a feeling
here that I can't give up. It's as though I have to stay."
  She spent a day just saying good-bye. The men were not notice-
ably upset by this. In fact, Melanie herself felt more shaken than
she'd expected. For Agram, she promised to write an adoring letter
for his collection. In turn, he drove her to his factory and gave her a

lamp that looked like a combination camel-antelope. The light bulbs came out of the humps.

Mordecai was a little bit more emotional, though not all that much. He told her to call him in Haifa should she change her mind about marriage, and for the first time he gave her his unlisted telephone number. Then he wished her good luck.

Early the following day, she waited by the bus stop with her bag. She gave her clothes to Shari, her books to Fuad, and took only the White Nile perfume, a notebook, her earrings, and a pen. The plan was to take the first bus that came by and get off in a place that seemed like home.